Worth a Thousand Words

Worth a Thousand Words

Brigit Young

Roaring Brook Press
New York

For my beloved dad, Ernest P. Young, who has been my trusted first pair of eyes on every piece of writing since my third-grade report on the Triceratops

A photograph is a secret about a secret. The more it tells you, the less you know.

—Diane Arbus

The world is full of obvious things which nobody by any chance ever observes.

—Sherlock Holmes, in Sir Arthur Conan Doyle's
The Hound of the Baskervilles

1

The Lost and Found

TILLIE GREEN STUDIED CONSTANTLY. NOT MATH, or English, but pictures. Pictures and pictures of everybody, scrutinizing their comings and goings, their forgotten moments, thoughtless mistakes, and ever-changing faces.

She arranged last week's photographs over the well-worn desk in her room. Ordering them based on chronology, she recounted the Monday-through-Friday lives of her classmates. She spotted Clay Johansson getting into an argument with the lunch lady about the quality of the tater tots. Next up was Mary Boyd, her eyes crinkled in a smile at Deshaun Washington as he read a poem at an assembly, oblivious to her adoration. And there, from Thursday, was the one Tillie had been looking for. It captured Tom Wilson laughing in the cafeteria in his oversized T-shirt, whispering something, his hands under the table along with Lauren Canopy's. It looked like they were passing a note of some kind. Or were they holding hands? Were their hands touching all the time now, only in secret? A photograph could hold many secrets, Tillie knew.

In the photo beneath it, taken on the same day, Tillie spotted Tom leaning against his locker reading something, his face scrunched up in concentration. As Tillie had first suspected, they must have been passing a note—*the* note. A love note, probably.

"I lost some . . . paper. A paper," he'd told her last week in an awkward panic. "I need it."

In the next photo, Tom was walking off, the note teetering out of his back pocket. Maybe it had fallen out shortly after, and if it was retrievable at all, it most likely sat in the recycling bin by Tom's locker on the third floor. The janitors were supposed to clear them every other day, but sometimes they neglected the bins by the stairwells.

One of her cases might be closed.

Satisfied, she grazed her fingers over more of her weekly spread: Cara Dale, laughing at something unseen as she played with her necklace; Ms. Martinez, the best teacher in the world teaching the best subject—art; and the beautiful and impeccably dressed Diana Farr, just a blur in the background of a classroom photo but somehow the star of it, even when out of focus.

Diana was the one who had designated Tillie the "Lost and Found"—the school's investigator, its finder of lost things. It had taken Diana over a year, all the way until the fall semester of seventh grade, to even notice Tillie. Tillie wasn't exactly of the same social status as Diana Farr. Tillie didn't even have a social status.

It had started with a typical Diana drama. One day, a few minutes before the first afternoon class began, Diana couldn't find her diamond bracelet.

When Tillie heard "I've lost them! I've lost the diamonds!" she remembered that just a few short hours ago she had noticed the bracelet's sparkle in one of her shots. She clicked through her morning's two dozen pictures. When she got to an image of Diana wearing it in the art room while she washed paint off her hands, Tillie went to retrieve it.

Coming back to Mr. Werner's classroom, Tillie murmured, "I've got it."

A hush fell over the class. Diana walked toward her.

"You last had it in art," Tillie said. "It must have fallen off in the sink when you washed your hands." She paused and shrugged. "It was still there. I saw it in my . . ."

Tillie nodded down to her camera, on its strap around her neck. "This."

Diana shrieked. She hugged Tillie, whose arms were stuck at her sides, and the class clapped.

"You guys!" Diana turned to the other kids. "Who needs that useless lost and found when we have Tils and her crazy camera?"

By the time the bell rang to start the next class, Tillie had existed for the first time.

Tillie's mom's voice broke her concentration—somehow it could boom and squeak simultaneously.

"Tillie! My love! School!"

"Okay, coming!"

She saved the new images she'd uploaded onto her laptop and shuffled all the printed pictures into her Lost and Found folder. One fell out and Tillie bent to pick it up.

It was from Sunday morning. Her dad stood in front of the kitchen window above the sink, drinking his morning coffee, his graying hair messy, staring at the bird feeder in the backyard. He had quietly watched the birds like this, Tillie was fairly certain, ever since the accident. Before, she remembered weekend mornings as full of pancakes and silly songs, the birds scared off by all the noise. But maybe she was just imagining things.

"I guess you're just not going to school today!" Her mom poked her head into Tillie's room. Eyeing Tillie's photographs, she added, "Seriously, get a move on, honey."

"I'm coming," Tillie repeated as she began to gather her things.

"And hey, make sure to text me when you're on your way home!"

Tillie sighed. Her mom always acted as if Templeton, Illinois, were Gotham City and not a small, boring college town in which the most dangerous thing Tillie could ever encounter would be an angry squirrel protecting its nuts. All the other kids got to hang out downtown after school, often until dark, getting hot chocolate and snacks on Main Street, but Tillie always had to head right home, or to physical therapy or a doctor's appointment. Not like she had anyone to get hot chocolate with, anyway. But it was the principle of the matter.

Tillie grabbed her coat and rushed out the door, her glasses sliding slightly down her nose, her backpack heavy on her shoulders, and her camera hanging from her neck, swinging in time with the drag-step rhythm of her walk as she made her way to the bus stop.

Tom Wilson's love note sat near the top of the overflowing recycling bin by the stairwell.

"Did you read it?" he asked as she handed it to him.

"No," she answered, already turning away.

"Okay, well—" he started.

She looked back at him.

"Never mind, Lost and Found," he muttered, and walked away.

"You're welcome," Tillie mumbled to Tom's back. *And tell Lauren Canopy "You're welcome," too,* she thought.

Tillie flexed her foot and released it a few times, like the physical therapists always told her to, and began to shuffle off to class. Her leg already hurt and it was only the beginning of the day. She noted some kind of commotion behind her but ignored it, focusing on balancing her walk and clicking shots of some new Sharpie graffiti on Alice Pierce's locker.

"Hey!" she heard from somewhere far off.

Someone had dropped an anatomy book on the ground. It lay flipped open to a picture of a skeleton. Tillie took a photo.

"Hey, wait up!" the same voice hollered again.

Tillie hardly registered the call behind her. She was

too busy noticing a circle of blue gum wads in the drinking fountain that reminded her of one of those old stone circles she had read about in history class. She snapped a shot of it.

"Lost and Found!" The voice had made its way to her, and Tillie felt a hand on her shoulder.

She stopped, turned, and hid a groan.

It was Jake Hausmann. She'd taken photos of him here and there, of course, but she'd gone out of her way to never have to speak to him.

"You're the Lost and Found, right?" he said. "You find stuff for people? They said to look for the girl that . . ." He blushed.

Tillie—as kids used to say back in elementary school before they were scolded for it—"walked funny." At first, for a few months, it was because of the back brace. Once that was off, it was the way her bones had healed, the way her legs had learned to get her around after all her body had been through.

Tillie's main doctor called her current walk "a triumph," usually adding, "It could've been much worse." Her mom said she was "so proud she'd come so far." The gym teacher said the whole thing was "a shame." The kids at school, most of them speaking in hushed tones they thought she couldn't hear—unless they were the mean ones and she got in their way in the hall or something—called it "freakish," "weird," or "super sad."

Back in elementary school, her classmates had been used to it. But once middle school started, and kids from all over town joined together for the sixth grade, it was a novelty for a while. And though most of them merely stared but never said anything, a few kids openly mocked her. One time, early in sixth grade, Tillie had noticed a group of kids laughing hysterically, holding their bellies, heads thrown back. She framed the image and locked onto the face of a laughing girl, nailing the focus. A perfect photo. But as she took the picture, a boy broke into the frame, ruining the shot. Through the lens, she saw that he was the source of all the hilarity. With his shoulders hunched over and his hair in his eyes, he dragged his leg and pretended to take pictures. As she dropped her camera against her chest and moved away as fast as she was able, the boy ended his impression and joined in the laughter, too, accepting pats on the back and high fives from those around him.

Now that boy stood before her, his pleading eyes fixed on hers.

"I need your help with something." He held her gaze. "It's important."

Everyone thought what they were missing was important.

"I have to get to class," Tillie snapped. It took her twice as long as the other kids to get down the hall and she was already late from lingering with her camera.

But then Jake grasped Tillie by the arm, and she fought the urge to flinch. She stopped.

His hand stayed on her. "No . . . I mean it."

Tillie stood still, feeling the heat of his hand, and looked Jake Hausmann up and down.

He was small—petite, even. A kid her mom might politely call a "late bloomer." He had a haircut one could only describe as ridiculous (shaggy-jagged, but a little too short in the back). He wore a shirt with Aragorn from Lord of the Rings on it, and his pants were too tight, revealing matchstick-thin legs. Despite all this, she knew that he was always in the center of every group of people he was around, just as he had been when she'd first spotted him.

"Please, Lost and Found. You have to help me. Just listen." He dropped his hold on her arm, and even though they were already standing close together, he took a small step toward her, staring right at her.

"Okay. What is it?" She tried to look away from his eyes, but despite their air of desperation, they were warm and wide. Somehow she had never noticed that in her photographs.

"I lost my dad," he said. "I need to find him."

2

Missing

"I DON'T LOOK FOR PEOPLE," TILLIE SAID, WALKING away. "Only things." She wished she could escape faster.

"But I heard you can find *anything*." Jake easily caught up with a small skip. "Figure stuff out."

Tillie arrived at her class and walked to her seat. She could see him outside the classroom door window, peeking in, fidgeting a little. She almost took a picture, but the teacher started lecturing, and Jake's face disappeared.

On the way home from school, he bothered her again.

"Hey!" he called to her as she was leaving. "Hey, you!"

Her bus idled, the last in line, and she sped up in an effort to ditch him. To do so, she had to thrust her left leg forward more forcefully, which emphasized the walk he once found so funny-looking.

Who loses their dad? A dad's not a bracelet. A dad's not a note. Who doesn't know where their dad is at every second, wishing him home from work or feeling his presence down the hall when you get ready for bed? A dad would have to be dead to be lost. Tillie shuddered.

"You can't ignore me forever, you know," he said, suddenly beside her.

"Can't I?" she replied under her breath. She knew just how easy it was to ignore someone. Or rather, to be ignored.

"I'm Jake," he said.

Tillie kept her gaze down on the sidewalk before her. About fifty more steps and she'd be at her bus.

"Do you always go by Lost and Found?" Jake continued. "Or do you find that insulting? People used to call me Supergirl in fourth grade, because I wore a cape to school. I thought it was red, but it was really pink. Ya see, I'm color-blind. I personally found the name insulting. Can't a person wear a pink cape? What, boys aren't allowed to wear pink or something? Pink is awesome!"

Tillie ignored him, but she couldn't deny that it was kind of nice to hear someone think out loud about how she might be feeling about something, about anything. And yeah, the pink cape story was kind of funny.

"Listen." The words poured out of him as he strode energetically beside her. "I think something weird is going on. My dad's been missing for three days now. He's not where they're telling me he is."

"What does that even mean, 'missing'?" Tillie grumbled. And who was "they"?

"Three days ago he drops me off at school and everything's good, right? That night, he isn't home for dinner, and my mom cooks it, and he's usually the one who cooks, so that's weird, but it's just one night, so I don't think much of it. Working late or something. And then he's not there in the morning, either. And my mom doesn't say anything. Okay, weird, but whatever. Early workday, maybe. But then it's movie night. Our movie night we have *every* week. And he would never, *never* miss a movie night. It was his idea! He *loves* movie night. But he's not home! So I ask my mom where he is and she says, 'Oh, I didn't tell you? He's out of town right now. In Toronto. For business.' For *business*? In *Toronto*? I mean, what is he, an international banker? The guy works in refrigeration sales! He's never taken a 'business trip' in his life! And on *movie night*?"

"You never know—" Tillie started, still forging ahead toward the bus, but Jake interrupted.

"But okay, fine. So then another day goes by and I still haven't heard from him. And *that* is weird."

"Why?" Tillie challenged, stopping and turning to him. It all sounded perfectly normal to her.

"It's just weird, okay?" he said. "We've had an ongoing game of D&D, just the two of us, since I was eight. We trade playlists and get into each other's music. Last year he took me to a Bob Dylan concert. The man was totally incomprehensible and, like, a lunatic, but still. It was awesome."

Jake spoke as if everyone would want to hear all he had to say, Tillie thought.

"So anyway, I decide to call him. And it goes straight to voicemail." Jake paused. "Let that sink in. No ring. Phone off," he said, enunciating each word. "The one time we were apart before—when my Zayde was in the hospital and Dad went to Chicago to see him—we talked every day. He called while caring for my sick grandfather, but he wouldn't call after three whole days away on some surprise 'business trip'? No. So I tell my mom I can't reach him and ask if he's called her, if we should worry. She says there's nothing to worry about, that he left his charger at home, so his phone died, but they've

14

been emailing and he's fine. So I think, 'Okay, then,' and I email him. He doesn't write back. And at this point, I start to think she might be lying for some reason."

"Did you look for the charger?" A simple mystery solved and Jake the Mocker would be on his way. If it was there, his mom was telling the truth, and there was his answer.

"Of course I did," Jake said. "He always keeps it plugged in next to his bed. And it's not there. So I search everywhere in the house, just in case. It's nowhere to be found. So why would she say that?"

In her peripheral vision, Tillie saw the bus filling up.

"Well," Tillie said as she moved away, "you just need to call his—"

"Work," Jake finished for her, not letting up, following. "I did. 'Could I speak with Dave Hausmann?' I ask, all professional. They transfer me to his private line. Voicemail. I call back and ask for his friend, his work buddy Jim. And guess what ol' Jim at the office says? First he goes, 'Oh, yeah, let me grab him,' and then Jim gets back on the phone and says, 'Oh, my mistake. He took the next couple weeks off. Vacation time.' Like . . . huh? Which is it—a business trip or a vacation? If he were on a business trip, wouldn't work know? And why would my mom say one thing and his coworker another? Look, someone is lying to me. I need to know why!"

"And what am I supposed to do, huh?" Tillie interrupted, hearing her own voice, a little louder than usual. "I take pictures. I'm not a *detective*."

Jake began to fidget again. He had a habit, she noticed, of scratching behind his right ear. It left a light layer of dandruff on his shoulder.

"But you are." He scratched away. "That's exactly what you are."

"No way," Tillie scoffed.

"You're *like* a detective. With your whole camera-toting, lurking-in-the-shadows, 'Lost and Found' thing."

Tillie paused. "'Lurking'? Thanks." The bus was a few yards away now, and she signaled to the driver to wait for her.

"No, I mean—I don't mean it like that," Jake said as she boarded.

"I don't think I can help you with this," Tillie said, stepping onto the bus.

She could feel his eyes on her as she left him standing there. It felt strange to be the one who was being watched.

That night, as she clicked through her shots from the day, she stopped on the one of Alice Pierce's locker. It had been covered in sloppily drawn little broken hearts. Who had done that, she wondered?

"Sweetie,"—Tillie heard her mom's voice from down the hall—"don't forget to do your exercises tonight, 'kay?"

Almost every night, her mom repeated this refrain. Sometimes the physical therapy exercises felt pointless, but her mom remained convinced that they would help reduce her pain and "abnormal gait," which was how the grown-ups around her referred to her limp.

"Just remember that you wouldn't be in as good a place as you are now if you hadn't been doing them this whole time, right from the beginning," her mom said whenever Tillie complained. Unfortunately, her mom happened to be right.

Tillie grabbed her ankle weights and dutifully went through her leg lifts. When she got to the resistance exercises, lying on her back and looping her band around her leg as she pushed against it, the band snapped in two. Tillie reached for another one, but she was all out.

"Mom!" she yelled from her room, still on her back. "Mom, my last band broke!"

No answer. Tillie pushed herself up off the floor and

went into her parents' bedroom, but her mom wasn't there.

Her dad sat in bed on top of the covers, his laptop on his thighs, his reading glasses pushed down to the tip of his nose.

"Hey," Tillie said.

"Oh," he said, his pitch rising in surprise at her presence, but not looking up. "Hey, Til. Good day?"

"Where's Mom?" Tillie asked.

"She just hopped on the phone with Aunt Kerry. What's up?" he said, still typing.

"My last band broke. Need someone to help with the resistance exercises," Tillie mumbled.

He lowered the screen of the laptop and glanced up at her. "Oh," he said again. His face dropped. "Um . . ." He looked around as if her mom would appear from thin air beside him and do the job herself.

Tillie began to lie down on the floor.

"Um, you know, Til, I've got to finish looking at this," he said. "Lots of work tonight."

"Any big scandals?" she asked, standing back up.

Her dad worked as the associate editor of the politics section of the local paper. Tillie loved hearing about the scandals, listening to him tell her mom about politicians' schemes and secrets. He got to cover stories in Chicago, too, which was where all the interesting stuff happened. "The salacious city!" her mom called it. Sometimes it seemed like his workday never ended.

"Nothing too exciting," he said with a little smile. "Anyway, can you wait for your mom? She won't be long."

"Okay, Dad."

He returned to whatever was so important on his computer.

Well, she could do them another time, once she had more bands. She went back to her room and her cameras, saving what she liked onto her laptop and clearing her memory card.

Performing her nightly ritual, Tillie set her cameras down on the shelf right across from her bed, where they spent their evenings, watching over her while she slept.

She placed them in order of size, starting with her smallest—a digital range finder that she carried around in her jacket pocket. She used it for clandestine photography, like when she propped the camera on a knee under her desk during class, or when she held it by her thigh, tilted upward, to capture a private moment between other kids. Then came her precious but resilient

DSLR, a piece of treasure found at a yard sale, the one she wore around her neck all day like armor. It had kept her company since the summer of fifth grade. At this point it felt like an extra limb. At the end of the row sat a bulky, medium-format film camera that used to be her mom's. It was too big to take to school, but perfect for playing around with at home. Every couple of weeks her mom took her to Walmart to get the film developed.

After laying her three beloved cameras in their resting spots, she stood back to admire them.

"Honey," she heard her mom yell, talking to the other 'honey' in the house, not her. "Tillie needs to do her resistance reps! *Can you please help her if she needs it?*"

A moment later her dad knocked on her door and said, "I've been summoned."

Tillie forced out an insincere laugh. "How'd she know?"

"Your mom knows all." He paused. "I think she just overheard us," he admitted.

Tillie lay on the floor and lifted her leg. Her dad crouched down and began the routine. They both looked up toward the ceiling, avoiding eye contact. He pushed against her leg, her leg pushed back against his hand. He increased the resistance with each lift. And then he increased it way too much.

"Ow, okay, too much, that hurts," she said as she felt a little pinch in her hip.

"What?" He responded as if he'd been elsewhere the whole time and was only now tuning in.

"That one hurt, Dad."

"Where? In your hip? Your leg?" he asked, frantic.

"Dad, it's fine. Just a little pinch. Let's keep going."

Her dad put his hand on his forehead, his usual move when he got upset or overwhelmed. He stood up. "Sorry, Til. Sorry."

"It's fine," she said, meaning it, lifting her leg to go again.

"Your mom's better at these . . . Maybe she should . . ." he muttered, heading toward the door without looking at her. "I, um . . . I really do need to work. I'm gonna see if your mom's off the phone."

And with that, he left.

Tillie stayed on the floor for a moment, the pinch still reverberating in her body, and then pulled herself up using the side of the bed. She could hear the faint sound of her mom's voice laughing on the phone with her aunt and the muffled click-clack of her dad's resumed typing down the hall.

Tillie tossed her weights aside, grabbed her laptop, put in a single headphone, and turned on one of the shows her parents caught every Sunday night that she wasn't allowed to see. By bedtime, the slight sting of the pinch in her hip was gone.

3

Happy Faces

TILLIE ATE LUNCH ALONE. ONCE A WEEK, MS.
Martinez allowed students to come to her room during lunch and work on their projects while they ate. But otherwise, Tillie parked herself at the end of the lunchroom's corner table, safe, secure, and solo in the cafeteria's nook.

There had been a time when she wasn't always alone. She and Sydney Welch and Zahreen Askari used to ride their bikes all around the neighborhood and play mermaids at every recess. But that was before the winter and spring when she had spent so much time in and out of the hospital that she had to be homeschooled. When she got back to school the next fall, her old friends didn't seem to understand what she could and couldn't do—she couldn't bike, she couldn't flap her imaginary fins. And Tillie could tell they were disappointed. She'd always been shy, but then seeing that disappointment on her friends' faces, or noticing the looks strangers gave her when they saw the chair or the walker or the brace or, for a while, the scars and bandages . . . that made her want to disappear. It became easier to stay indoors at recess, to tell her mom to turn Sydney and Zahreen away when they knocked on her door to hang out.

Everything was easier to manage alone.

As Tillie dug into her plate of tater tots, Jake Hausmann plopped down next to her.

"What's up?" he said.

As he moved in beside her, Tillie saw a dozen people wave at him from across the room, and he flashed a huge, toothy smile back. It was a wonder Jake didn't have braces yet.

Out of habit, Tillie picked up her camera and within a split second she took a handful of pictures of his pack of friends.

"Can I see?" Jake asked.

Tillie just sighed. She rolled her eyes and went back to her food.

"Okay, then. Guess not." He shrugged. "Hey, how do

you not get into trouble for that?" he asked her, motioning with his head toward the camera.

"Yearbook," she said to her feet, telling her usual half-truth. The school had a policy against taking photographs of anybody without their consent. In the early months of middle school the hall monitors had taken away Tillie's camera every week. She'd even begun to resort to phone photography (which was more discreet but less satisfying), and they had caught her doing that, too. But then Ms. Martinez had asked if she could contribute some of her photos to the yearbook, which Ms. Martinez ran. After that, when a hall monitor or teacher told Tillie she couldn't take pictures, she simply said, "It's for yearbook," sometimes adding, "You can ask Ms. Martinez." And then, just to be safe, she'd hobble away from the reprimanding adult, exaggerating her limp as much as she could, adding a couple of groans to each pull of the leg, and slowing her pace to that of an overheated sloth. At this point no one even bothered her about it anymore.

Only a few of the photos actually ended up in the yearbook, but Jake didn't need to know that. Why couldn't he just go away?

"So check it out," Jake said, tossing something beside her tray and taking a bite of pizza.

Tillie picked it up. A passport. "David G. Hausmann," it read, next to an unflattering photograph of a pale, reddish-blond, middle-aged man.

"Is this . . . ?" Tillie flipped through it, not knowing exactly what she was looking for.

"Yup. That's my dad." Jake chewed as he spoke. "*Not* in Toronto. Or else he'd need *this*." He smiled a smug grin. "What's the explanation for that, huh?"

Okay, yes, it was strange that his mom would say his dad was in Canada, but his passport was at home. It was a little off that his dad had left unexpectedly and appeared to be unreachable. But there was also probably a perfectly ordinary reason for it. "Maybe your parents, you know . . ." Tillie faltered, "miscommunicated."

Jake dropped his pizza, looked her right in the eye, and said, "Is that why someone followed me to school today? Because my parents 'miscommunicated'?"

Tillie began to blow this off, but then she saw that his eyes were darting back and forth as if looking to see if someone was following him right then. He seemed genuinely nervous. "Wait. Why do you think—"

Jake cut her off. "Look," he said, shaking his head, "you found my buddy Ian's soccer cleats and Aiden's permission slip right before the Chicago trip. And yeah, those are *things*, not *people*, but it's impressive."

26

The memory of him mimicking her walk flashed through Tillie's mind.

"Isn't it boring being so detective-y and not having any real detective work to do? Maybe finding Cara Dale's lost left earring or Hailey Granito's winter coat is exciting to you, but it all sounds kind of tedious to me, to be honest."

"Not a detective," Tillie said through clenched teeth.

"Okay, fine. So you're an artist, then. Same problem. This school doesn't exactly lend itself to Mona Lisa–level material, am I right?" He laughed. "So why not help me out with something a little . . . *bigger* than Hansberry Middle School?"

Tillie wanted to respond: "Well, you're kind of right, I would love some new subjects for my photographs," or, "Yeah, I am curious about the bigger mysteries behind the people in my pictures." Actually, she *really* wanted to respond: "Why would you want the help of someone who you think walks funny?" She stayed quiet instead.

"And this is definitely bigger," Jake continued. "This car stuff . . . Man. You never think anything high-level bad is going to happen to you, you know? And then it does. And not just bad, but action-movie bad. Scary, even." Jake shook his head and looked off into the distance. "Life-changing."

What was he talking about?

"Okay." Tillie gave in. "Who followed you? What's going on?"

Jake leaned in toward her and spoke quickly. "Okay. I know you think this is ridiculous, but it's just *true* that two days in a row now, on my walk to school, a blue Chevy—*the same blue Chevy*—has rolled along a little ways behind me for two blocks. I didn't mention it yesterday because I thought I was being paranoid. But then, today, it happened again. Making the turns I make, slowing down just enough so I might not notice . . . This morning I took out my cell and put it on selfie mode, like a mirror, and tried to see who was driving—"

"Good thinking." Tillie couldn't help but cut in.

"But once again no luck. I should've just turned around and run toward it," Jake chastised himself. "The big question is: Why would someone follow me? That's what you were going to ask, right? What does that have to do with my dad?"

Tillie's silence served as an admission.

"The answer is, I don't know. I have some ideas, but I don't know."

And it could all be in his head, she thought.

"This is what I *do* know: My dad suddenly goes out of town. To Canada, supposedly. But his passport is at home.

His phone isn't on, but it looks to me like he took a charger with him. My mom is saying one thing, his work another. And then a car starts following me—yeah, yeah, I know, it sounds paranoid"—he cut Tillie off before she had the chance to say anything—"but it's not only that. The day after he leaves, I start getting calls from a blocked number. But when I answer, whoever it is hangs up. Now, why would *that* happen?"

Tillie didn't know what to say. It sounded like it could all be in his head, sure. But if it wasn't, if these things held any truth, it was pretty creepy.

"Look," Jake whispered, leaning closer. She could smell the pizza on his breath. "Maybe he left out of nowhere because he had to run away from something. Maybe whoever followed me, whoever called, is looking for him. Maybe he's in serious trouble." Jake began to speak even faster, as if letting Tillie get a word in would make it all fall apart. "Or maybe he saw something he shouldn't have seen. A crime. Someone doing something at work that they shouldn't have been doing. Something illegal, maybe? Maybe he's hiding out somewhere, waiting for it all to be resolved. Maybe my mom knows, and she's trying to protect me from all of it, and that's why she's lying."

He's had too many movie nights, Tillie thought. "I don't know . . ."

Jake's friends yelled his name and he looked up, smiling broadly, like he didn't have a care in the world, and motioned "one sec." Then he turned to Tillie, his face brighter than it had been a moment ago, as if he were suddenly aware he was on a stage and had an audience.

"I really just don't know . . ." Tillie repeated. "Isn't it possible your parents are in a fight? Or there are just . . . 'domestic' issues or something? And the car and the phone are just . . . in your head?"

Jake leaned over his backpack and pulled out a big blue book with a gold floral design on its cover.

"I knew you might say that. So I think you should look at these." Jake opened up the book. "I think they'll be helpful. I think you'll see what I see."

Before Tillie could protest, he had pushed her tray out of the way and shoved the book right in front of her. Her eyes fell upon an array of happy faces decorating worn, yellowed pages: beaming faces, faces with tongues out, faces talking over piles of food on a beautifully set table. In the first pages, there was a woman in almost all of them. She had velvety brown hair in loose, wavy curls, and a gap-toothed smile that matched the shape of Jake's. The man in the pictures had strawberry-blond hair, wore glasses, and was too thin. In the first pictures he seemed to be kissing the woman all the time. In front of the Lincoln Memorial he had his face buried in her hair as she giggled, her head thrown back. In one, he had his lips puckered on hers as they sat in front of a lit birthday cake, spreading frosting on her cheek with a finger.

Tillie couldn't help but smile at it.

As the pictures went on, the woman grew a big, round belly, and the kisses started to move away from her face and toward her belly button. Soon Jake arrived and the man transformed into a master of goofy camera faces. In a lot of the pictures, Jake looked upward and cracked up hysterically at the crossed eyes and stuck-out tongue of the man holding him. The pictures started to be dominated by the man and Jake. Page after page depicted the man and Jake laughing everywhere they went—at Cubs games, at Millennium Park, wrestling on the beach, playing board games.

Tillie flipped through the album in silence. Everyone was smiling so much. It was like none of them had ever been sad.

When she finished, she saw that Jake was still looking right at her. Once again, his eyes were wide. And they seemed to be begging her.

"See? See how happy we are? I know my dad," Jake said. "My dad would never just *leave*. Not without talking to me. *Something* is wrong. Will you please help me?"

Tillie sighed. He was impossible to say no to.

"Fine," she said, averting her eyes from the photo album, from Jake. "I'll look for him."

He whispered, "Yes!" and broke into a little victory dance, lifting his hand for a high five—until she stopped him with:

"But I work alone."

4

A Boy on the Phone

THE DAY TILLIE GOT HER FIRST CAMERA WAS THE day she lost her soccer ball.

Everybody had gathered for her ninth birthday, the first after the accident. She had just gotten out of the casts and the wheelchair, which was cause itself for celebration, but the doctors' appointments were just beginning. In the car accident, something had happened to her spine and hip, and it was going to make her leg not work properly, ever again, and something had happened to her dad, and it made him sad, and that was all she could understand then. It was only later Tillie recognized that while she blamed the ice and the tree and the metal for what had happened to her, her dad blamed his eyes and his hands.

"Your dad is just going through a time," Tillie's mom used to say to her when she'd ask why Dad didn't like pushing her around in the wheelchair.

"Is he scared of wheels?" Tillie had asked.

Sometimes there were questions her mom simply did not answer. There was a whole world of mysteries in her family's small, one-floor home.

Her birthday was in May, the perfect time for outdoor parties. For her last two birthdays, her dad had organized a soccer game with their neighbors, her grandparents, and her cousins, and so, after Tillie had blown out the candles, she asked her dad when they were heading to the park to play. Instead of answering her, Tillie's dad sighed and stayed quiet, as he had been all day, as he had been when everyone else was singing "Happy Birthday" at full voice.

"Let's go after we eat," her grandpa answered for him. He spoke to Tillie but looked right at her dad when he added, "You can be the referee, kiddo."

When everyone was leaving, Tillie heard her grandpa and dad talking in the kitchen.

"Come on," her grandpa was saying. "Look at her. She's smiling. She's fine."

"She's in pain, Dad. Constantly. She can't do regular stuff, like ride a bicycle, or—"

"Just snap out of it," her grandpa said gruffly.

"Dad, just leave," her dad said. "I'm not going."

"Kid, at some point you'll have to accept that accidents happen. You didn't put that ice on the road. Anyone could have been driving."

"Stop it, Dad. Stop it," her dad interrupted, with a sharpness that was followed by silence.

Before the game began, Tillie's grandpa handed her a box. It wasn't wrapped. It was just cardboard, its sides closed up with duct tape.

As she ripped the tape off, her grandpa said, "Someone needs to watch this game carefully so we know what really happened. You know your cousin Aaron can be a wily goalie."

Inside the box sat something that looked like a little robot: gray rectangles stacked upon one another with a black circle of glass in the middle that reminded Tillie of a cyclops eye.

"It's a Polaroid camera," her grandpa said with a smile. "Had it for years. Got it fixed up the other day. They told me it should work just fine now, and that we can get more film for it on eBay. Give it a try."

Tillie turned the camera toward her face to look at it more closely and a flash of light blinded her. She had accidentally taken a picture of herself. She laughed.

From the bottom of the camera, a tiny slip of plastic paper shot out. It began to transform into shapes and colors right before her eyes, and slowly the outline of her own delighted face began to appear; her hazel eyes smiled and the freckles on her nose reflected the sun like brown sparkles. She had taken her first photograph.

"Try again," her grandpa said. "Point your camera at something. Something out there." He motioned to the landscape of the park.

Tillie lifted the viewfinder to her eye. She landed on a towering tree with sprawling roots. When the image printed and came to life before her, Tillie gasped.

"You have a good eye," her grandpa said, looking over her shoulder at the picture. "I figured that'd be the case." He patted her back. "Try to get a shot of me scoring the winning goal." He winked at her and ran off to start the game.

That day, Tillie caught every moment she could: a high five between her cousin and grandpa, her aunt's laughter, her grandpa running, her mom posing with the ball after scoring. At nightfall, Tillie flipped through all her Polaroids and felt like she had made a million paintings with just her eye and the tip of her pointer finger, like magic. As she leaned out the window to try to take a Polaroid of the starry Illinois sky, she saw that someone had put the soccer ball out on the curb by the trash.

It was her dad's job to take out the garbage.

Since that birthday, Tillie had collected several more cameras, but had never seen a soccer ball in the house again.

"Honey? There's a boy on my phone asking for you! Did you hear me? There's a boy on the phone!" Tillie heard outside her door, along with a series of frenzied-sounding knocks.

Tillie was busy ignoring her homework and playing around with her film camera. She had been trying to capture the way the crescent moon sat in the sky. The word "boy" caused her to take the shot at the wrong moment, and she was sure the effect would be ruined.

Before she even had a chance to say it was okay, her mom came into her room, holding the cell phone against her chest like a baby doll. She had her palm over the mouthpiece and she mouthed the words without sound:

There's a boy on the phone!

Tillie grabbed the phone and shut the door before her mom could give one of her signature concerned looks.

She slammed the phone against her ear, and hissed out, "What are you doing calling my *mom*?"

"Hey! How'd you know it was me? Your mom seems nice." Jake's voice sounded upbeat, pleased.

"How did you even get her number?" Tillie asked.

"What do you mean? School directory, of course," he said, as if it were obvious.

Tillie had never used the school directory.

"I asked around about your full name, *Matilda Green*. And the directory has all the parents' numbers. I meant to ask for yours earlier. Hey, can you text it to me from this phone or something?"

Tillie hesitated. She went to the door and opened it a crack to see if her mom was eavesdropping, but the hallway was empty. "Okay, fine," she said. "And it's Tillie. So what do you want now?"

"My mom was looking over bank statements tonight," Jake whispered.

"Huh?"

"Earlier tonight I saw her poring over some papers,

and normally I'd assume it was just work, but she looked . . . extra stressed. And my mom is like Clint Eastwood or something, I mean, she's tough. Stoic. But there she was—rubbing her head and stuff, sighing. Anyway, when she went to the bathroom, I did a total ninja move and flew over the couch, checked what she was looking at, and saw the papers were *bank statements*." He paused as if waiting for Tillie to respond with shock. "*Family finances*, Tillie. That's pretty telling, don't you think? Like maybe my dad is in some kind of trouble and we need money to help him?"

"I guess," Tillie said. "Isn't it almost tax season or something, though?"

Jake groaned. "Tillie, these things are *cumulative*, okay? Taken one at a time they're not a big deal, but add them all together! Hey, I think I know the first place we should investigate," he continued.

"I told you earlier, I do this all . . ."

"Alone," Jake interrupted. "I know. But the thing is . . . my presence is kind of crucial in this. It's my dad, after all . . ."

Tillie heard some grumbling and shuffling on the other end of the line, and then Jake yelled out in a singsong voice as perky as a cheerleader's, "I'm okay, Mom!

It's fine! Yeah, I'm on with a friend from school! Sorry about that," he said back into the phone, sounding like the real Jake again. "I'm trying to act like everything is even better than normal. I could tell she sensed my suspicion about Toronto when she told me. But if she's lying to me about something, the more innocent she thinks I am, the more I can actually uncover. And it's working. She never would've left those bank statements out for me to look at if she knew that I knew something was up."

"Look," Tillie said, "I'm not 'on call' here. I don't know what you think I do with my time, but it's not all Lost and Found."

She could hear the sad lie in her voice and was sure he could, too. And, truthfully, she'd been thinking about Jake's dad all afternoon. Despite his wild, unrealistic tales about all of it, he was probably right that there was *something* there that needed unraveling.

Tillie still heard noise in the background, but it sounded like more than one person. "It's hard to hear you."

"My mom and I have both been watching TV a lot since Dad disappeared," he said. "He's the talker in the family. Without him around, we just binge-watch and play on our phones next to each other."

"He's the talker?" Tillie heard herself asking. She tried to imagine her dad being chatty and couldn't.

She headed toward her laptop and absentmindedly clicked through the photos from the day.

"Oh, yeah. He can tell jokes like nobody's business. Hey, here's one of my favorites: You can't run in a campground. Only ran." He waited. Tillie didn't answer. "Why?" he continued. "Because it's always past tents!"

Jake laughed and Tillie couldn't help but join in a little. "Grammar humor," she said.

Tillie clicked on the photo she'd taken earlier that day of Jake's friends across the room in the cafeteria. A couple of them looked surprised that he was over there, talking to her, while the others didn't even seem to notice.

"Yeah. Anyway," Jake went on, "weird about the bank statements, right?"

Tillie wished he'd ask her what she did besides Lost and Found. She'd think of something.

"That really could be random."

"I was thinking," Jake said, ignoring her dissent, "since my dad was so funny and everybody loved him, maybe we could go talk to a couple of his friends at work tomorrow. Maybe they *do* know where he is—maybe it's only Jim who's lying. Or maybe Jim really thinks my dad is using his vacation time—though I doubt it—but we could chat him up and get some clues. Collect evidence. Or however it is you find people."

Things, not people.

"And then we could go somewhere he might have gone. Like the happy places from the pictures. I was thinking of the house he and my mom first lived in together, on Maple Street. If he's hiding somewhere, on the run from somebody or something, if that's what's going on, I know that's where he'd go to leave me a clue if he had a chance. I mean, I know it's unlikely—other people live there now. But still, we're short on leads, right? Plus," Jake added, his words slowing and softening, "I know it sounds dumb, but whenever we'd drive by that house, he'd always talk about moving back to that neighborhood someday. He loved it there." He paused. "I'm really worried, Tillie," he said.

A moment of quiet passed between them. Tillie could hear his breath.

"So could we meet tomorrow?" he asked.

"Okay." The word tumbled out. "But I'm always supposed to come home right after school," Tillie heard herself saying, as if it were a disembodied voice. It was odd to be making after-school plans with someone who wasn't her mom. "So I don't know how I could get around that."

"Hmm . . ." Jake said, and she imagined him doing something silly like stroking a fake goatee. "I'll have this figured out by tomorrow. Your parents won't have a clue, trust me. And hey," he added, "think of how many photos you'll get. And not just of dirty hallways and lunch lines, but, ya know, the big, bad world."

Tillie sighed. "Fine."

"Great!" he nearly yelled. "After school! Tomorrow!"

Hearing Jake's voice, away from the noise of the hallway and directed solely at her, Tillie could suddenly picture him in pajamas in front of the TV, or reading comic books alone, or answering his mom's questions about his day over dinner, not just goofing off for all the kids at school. It was so strange she almost giggled.

After texting Jake her number and then immediately deleting the text so her mom wouldn't see it, Tillie got up to hand her mom's phone back to her and to tell her to please never say anything like "There's a boy on the phone" again. As she opened the door she saw her mom standing right outside of it, pretending she hadn't been listening, trying to look like she'd just been heading to her own room, but she'd obviously come sneaking back after Tillie had checked the hallway.

Tillie glared at her.

"Who was that, honeypie?" she asked with a smile. Her mom looked so much like a mom sometimes.

With a step-drop, step-drop, step-drop, Tillie shuffled right past her down the hall to find her dad.

As if on cue, he walked out of the bathroom with a book in hand, absorbed, as her mom said to her back, "What's with all this about lost and found? Did you lose something? Was it those gloves? Please don't tell me I need to worry about your hands getting cold this March!"

Her dad didn't look up from his reading and walking.

Tillie turned to him, shifting her weight toward her good leg. They all stood crammed together in the hallway between their rooms.

"Dad! I got a phone call, and Mom listened to my conversation through the door!"

"Hmm? Wait, what'd you say? What's the problem?" her dad asked, as if he hadn't heard her.

"She was on the phone with a *boy*," her mom said to her dad, but really to her. "He called on *my* phone. I just wanted to make sure everything's okay. I—"

"Mom! He's just from school! It was homework! It's . . . *normal!*" Tillie sputtered. She looked toward her dad.

He let out a tiny exhalation, the ghost of a laugh. "I'm sure it was just homework," he said to her mom. "No need to worry," he added, and he left the conversation, back to his book, into the bedroom, door shut for the night.

Tillie's mom gave her a look of apology, but whether it was for her dad's indifference or the eavesdropping, Tillie didn't know. She gave her mom one last frown, turned away, and shut herself in her room.

Why wouldn't you have to worry, Dad? Tillie thought. *You don't have to worry about a boy liking your weird, limping daughter? That's funny to you?*

A surge of pain shot down her leg that was so bad she had to lie down. Resigned to a night of discomfort, she did her usual B-grade job on her math and geography homework, hating every minute of it.

That night, before turning off the lights, Tillie looked toward her nightstand at her now-broken Polaroid camera and, sitting beside it, the framed shot of her grandpa playing soccer. It had been one of the last times she had ever seen him.

She closed her eyes and wished that photographs could be time machines. As she fell asleep, she remembered the perfect family photos that Jake had shown her that afternoon, and how he probably knew exactly how that wish felt.

5

Hiding Something

THE NEXT AFTERNOON AT LUNCH, JAKE presented Tillie with his plan for her cover story. Tillie would pretend to join a school club, a club any parent would be happy about their kid joining. "Somewhere you make friends *and* you learn—a parent's dream," Jake had said. "Like . . . Salsa Dancing or Meditation Club?" Jake visibly shivered. "All that sitting still and breathing . . . Yikes."

She shook her head at both suggestions. "Salsa? Really?" She motioned with her head down to her leg. It's not as if she couldn't do some Tillie version of the salsa; it's just that it would physically hurt. And because of that, her mom would never stand for it. But Jake couldn't understand that.

"Oh. Right."

They decided on Art Club—vague, but believable enough. It would meet on Mondays and Thursdays. Tillie wasn't sure it would work at all, but when she texted her mom that Ms. Martinez had asked her to join the new Art Club, and it started that day, so she had to stay at school and would take the town bus home, she was surprised to find that her mom responded, **Ok!!!! Sounds amazing, honey!!! Have so much fun!!!**

"See?" Jake said. "Moms love clubs."

Apparently, Jake's mom didn't care much about where he went right after school as long as he told her his general plans. It was his dad who'd been the one who paid attention. But he felt he needed a cover story, too, just in case, so he would also be joining the imaginary club.

"So you told her Ms. Martinez runs fake Art Club?" Jake asked between bites of pizza.

"Yeah," Tillie said, putting French fries into her mouth with one hand and flipping through pictures on her camera with the other.

"Ms. Martinez loves me," Jake went on, seemingly unable to end a conversation quickly. "Told my parents at the parent-teacher conferences that my work in class is 'original.' You better believe I kept that one in my brain's compliment file, along with my rabbi telling me I'm one of his favorite kids, and all the times my mom called me handsome." He wiggled his eyebrows up and down at Tillie.

Tillie choked a little on her French fry. "You're a total weirdo! Your 'brain's compliment file'?!"

"Hey, I'm very special," he said. "Everyone in my immediate family says so. Though, to be fair, 'original' probably really meant 'his-drawings-look-like-chicken-scratch-and-I-need-a-nice-way-to-say-so.' Ha!" He laughed with the food in his mouth showing. "And she's the prettiest teacher I've ever seen. Makes Ms. Rudolph look like a goblin. Though that's not hard. Did they have to find someone who was alive during the Civil War to teach us about the Civil War or something?" Jake chuckled again. Then he patted Tillie on the back, a little too hard, and went off to his friends.

After meeting at the flagpole, they began walking down Hillberry Street toward Lake Avenue, where Jake's dad's office building was.

"So here are my two theories," Jake said as they began their long trek.

Just like everybody who walked with Tillie, Jake's

pace kept him slightly in front of her, but he seemed to remember every few steps that he needed to slow down.

"I think he might have seen something, something really bad, and has to lay low for a while, even from me. Ya know, like in that old movie *Enemy of the State*."

"I've never seen it."

"The main guy ends up in possession of some footage of a political assassination, and the whole government is out to get him," Jake told her matter-of-factly.

"Oh, that's—" Before Tillie could say "ridiculous," Jake jumped in.

"I know, I know, obviously it's not *that*. But I'm talking on a smaller level. Okay, so one time my dad told me—it was probably a year or two ago—that there was a guy at work who would steal the office supplies sometimes. The guy got into a lot of trouble. Dad laughed it off at the time, but maybe that guy did something even worse recently. Stole something big. My dad saw it. The guy couldn't stand to lose his job, maybe he's a psycho or something, so he threatened Dad. Or our family. My dad had to cut off all ties for a while. Worst-case scenario, the guy hurt him or something." Jake winced and then shook his head. "No, no, probably he's not hurt, definitely not. But anyway, that's one option."

"Hmm . . ." Tillie said. "That all sounds like a little bit of a stretch, don't you think?"

A squirrel leapt across the cold, dead grass on a lawn. Tillie lifted up her camera and captured its scramble to an oak tree.

"You really love that camera, huh?" Jake's eyes followed the squirrel, and his face tilted toward the high branches against the sky.

Another squirrel came out of the bushes and ran in the exact same path that the first squirrel had, following it up the bark. Instead of answering him, Tillie took another picture.

"I should get a pet squirrel." Jake grinned. "Oh man, that would be so awesome. I'd be that guy. The pet-squirrel guy."

Tillie smirked, releasing her camera as the squirrels continued their chase in the treetops. "Is 'awesome' really the word for being a 'pet-squirrel guy'?" she said. "Alright, so what's your other theory?"

"Huh?" he said, and Tillie saw that he had been glancing behind them, as if on the lookout for the maybe-imaginary blue car. "Oh, yeah. Well, if you think that one's a stretch, you're going to have a really tough time with this one . . . But stick with me here."

"Okay . . ."

"What if my dad was"—he paused and inhaled a big breath, then let it out—"kidnapped?"

Tillie cocked an eyebrow. "*Kidnapped?*"

"Unlikely, I know, but there's some circumstantial evidence to back up this theory, and it's a doozy."

"'It's a doozy'?" Tillie couldn't help but interject. "Why do you talk like my grandpa sometimes?"

Jake shrugged. "Movie nights usually include some classics, ya know? They talked a lot better in the olden days. More colorful language."

Tillie shook her head and laughed quietly. He was absurd.

"Look, we inherited some money last year when Zayde died."

"Oh," Tillie gulped. "I'm sorry—"

"It's fine, it's fine, it was really sad, but it's fine," Jake brushed her off. "Anyway, it wasn't a lot, but a good amount. And I'm sure Dad told his buddies at work about it. No question. And maybe *they* thought it was a lot. Maybe someone was desperate, and needed Bubbe and Zayde's cash. Maybe that's why my mom's lying, looking at bank statements, and why everyone's got a different story for where he is."

"Okay," Tillie said, feeling her backpack get much heavier as the walk continued, the familiar throb beginning in her hip and leg. "But isn't it possible your dad is just having a midlife crisis or something?" Maybe his dad was one of those guys who bought Ferraris with money he didn't have or went on long hikes in the wilderness out of nowhere. Her dad had written about politicians who did that kind of stuff. "Like maybe your mom and him were having money problems? Fighting about it?"

She remembered her parents' arguments over medical bills and cringed inwardly.

"Oh, come on, but what parents don't fight, right?" Jake said. His pace quickened, putting him a few steps ahead of her, so he raised his voice as he spoke.

"Okay, but . . ." Tillie went on, badgering him a little, "it *is* the most reasonable explanation for someone not showing up at home. Or at work."

"Look, my parents are an opposites-attract situation, okay? Fire and ice. Gimli and Legolas. Artist and scientist."

"I get it."

"For the record, my dad's Gimli. And plus, my dad and I talk about *everything*. Even if there *were* a big problem or something, he'd talk to me about it! Look, I know you don't want to believe something really bad happened, and trust me, I don't either."

Tillie threw him a skeptical look.

"I don't!" Jake had a bit of a gallop to his walk, Tillie noticed. Everything about him was hyper, excitable. Even his voice. When he got worked up, he chirped. "I just know something bad *did* happen! Does a fight or a midlife crisis explain the blocked number? The car? All the . . . *weirdness*? Just trust me, when we get to his office, you'll see. You'll see I'm not so crazy."

Jake wore his backpack with the straps so loose that it hung down to the top of his pants, and it bounced against him as he strolled.

They left the brick houses and narrow sidewalks with the occasional car rolling by and arrived at Lake Avenue. The volume of the world turned up.

Tillie felt her leg clench tight. All the cars made her nervous.

"You okay?" she heard Jake say over the vrooms of motors, and she saw he had slowed down to walk beside her.

Tillie turned to him, the light March wind blowing her hair out of her face, the chill adding a slight mist to her glasses, and she noticed his eyes once again: Round. Sincere. It was hard to look into them and see the boy who had made fun of her in sixth grade.

"What is it?" Jake asked.

She tilted her head toward her feet and let out a sigh. "I hope we're almost there," she said. "I have to do some stuff for Diana Farr and I have a million pictures to go through for that and a lot of homework. So let's make this quick." She tried to speed up, which always made her limp more pronounced, but she really needed to escape Jake's stare.

Jake's dad worked in a cubicle in the sales department of a company that sold commercial refrigerators and freezers. Jake said he used to have a job he liked better, back when they lived in their house on Maple Street, but he got laid off.

"But it's not so bad, my dad says," Jake told her as they made their way into the building. Jake acted as if he'd been there a million times before, just hopping on the elevator and heading to the floor of his dad's company's offices like it was second nature. "He says his buddies make it kind of fun, actually. Although, for all we know, one of these 'buddies' is threatening my dad, or—"

"Are we allowed up here?" Tillie interrupted as the elevator doors opened. In front of them stood a glass wall and two floor-to-ceiling glass doors leading to a few dozen cubicles filling a vast off-white space. Everyone looked extremely busy. And grumpy. As inconspicuously as possible, she took a couple of pictures of the general boredom before her.

"Oh, yeah," Jake said. "I come here a lot. Dad lets me stop by and we chat for a bit as he gets coffee or whatever. One time I went out on an on-site visit with him. Some grocery store thinking of upgrading their cooling systems. That was kinda boring, to be honest. Sometimes I come after school and he leaves early and we head home together. I know these guys."

Jake went right up to the door.

"It's always locked," he said to Tillie as he began to wave to someone inside. "They'll let us in."

Jake caught the eye of a man with a brown suit, a receding hairline, and a pained look on his face. The man waved back to Jake, looked side to side, and came their way.

"This is the guy who told me my dad was on vacation," Jake whispered through his teeth.

When the man got to the door he opened it, but instead of letting them in, he came out and shut the door behind him.

"Jim!" Jake put his hand up to give the guy a high five, and the man gave in as he glanced at Tillie, before turning back quickly to Jake.

"Hey," the man—Jim—said.

Tillie couldn't believe Jake knew the names of his dad's coworkers. She'd never been to her dad's or mom's work. Well, she used to visit her mom, who was a secretary at the front desk of the English department at the local college, back when she was little. But not in a long time. Jake wasn't exaggerating when he said he and his dad were so close.

"Here to see Dad," Jake announced, moving past the man to grab the door handle.

Jim didn't step aside to let him in.

"Oh, hey, buddy, your dad's still out using his vacation leave," Jim said. He glanced toward the cubicles behind him and then back toward Jake and Tillie several times, shifting from one foot to the other. "Sorry," he added.

Jake threw Tillie a raised eyebrow.

"Well, that's weird," Jake said. "He hasn't been at home either, Jim, and my mom says he's in Canada for work."

Tillie stood close to Jake's side, holding her small range finder by her thigh and snapping pictures, angling the lens up toward the man and the office.

Jim glanced back at the cubicles again. "Oh my gosh, you're right," he said, smacking his own forehead lightly. "I'm confusing everybody's schedules over here. No, no, he's in Canada, that's right."

"Huh," Jake said.

"But I've got to get you away from the door, buddy," Jim went on. "You better head out. Company policy. Can't let you in during work hours."

"That's not true," Jake insisted, a touch of despair creeping into his voice. "I come here after school all the time."

Jim paused. "Well, your dad was with you then."

"Ah, okay, okay." Jake nodded, pretending to let it all go. "Yeah, I guess I'll just see him at home when he gets back from . . . from wherever. But hey, let me just go grab some stuff for him. He left some things at his desk my mom needs. I'll bring the stuff home."

That was smart, Tillie thought. There could be clues there. And if Jim wouldn't take his eyes off them, she could secretly take photos of his desk and they could decipher what they saw in detail later.

Jim smacked his lips grimly. "Kid . . ." he said, trailing off.

"Well, I mean . . ." Jake was not deterred. "Aren't you his friend? Don't you want us to have his stuff we need?"

Jim looked back into the office once again. He ran his fingers through his meager amount of hair. He moved side to side slightly like he had to go to the bathroom. Then he shook his head and burst out, "Jake! Just let it go, okay?"

Jake surrendered. "Okay, Jim. Okay. I don't wanna cause any trouble."

"I don't know what to tell you," Jim said, lowering his voice again. "But . . . I just can't let you in. So, well, I'll see you."

Jim turned, opened the transparent door, and shut it behind him. Once the door was closed, he gave a sad, closed-mouth smile to Jake and Tillie and walked away, combing his fingers through his hair over and over again before he disappeared into a cubicle in the back of the room.

As they burst out of the building and back onto the sidewalk, Jake raced ahead of Tillie, stopping himself and heading back every few steps to speak to her.

"Something was up," he said, his voice strident. "Something was definitely up."

Tillie, tagging along behind, clicked through the pictures she had taken, and from the looks of them, she agreed. As the images progressed, Jim looked more and more uncomfortable, his anxiety documented by the small dent in his forehead, the tiny drop of sweat between his eyebrows, and the dozens of shots of him looking back toward the room behind him, as if checking on something.

"He was lying, right? He was lying about *something*." Jake hurried on, away from the building. "Right? You have to understand, Tillie. Jim is my dad's good friend. They play poker together. If he truly thought my dad was out on 'vacation time' and I told him he wasn't home or on vacation . . . he'd be worried about my dad. But he wasn't. At all."

"Could he have actually been mistaken about where your dad was?" Tillie asked.

"Yeah, sure!" Jake nearly yelled. "But then why would he act so weird?" Jake shook his head and said to himself, "He was scared of something. He seemed . . . angry or guilty or something."

Jake was right. Tillie kept one eye on Jake to make

sure she didn't fall too far behind him and one eye on the images on her tiny screen. As Jake turned the corner onto Maple Street, Tillie spotted her first real clue.

"Hey, Jake, wait up!" she called out.

He hustled back to her.

"Look at this," she said, still catching her breath from trying to keep up with him.

Their heads bent close together toward the billions of colored pixels that made up the photo before them.

"Look at the man back there." Tillie zoomed in on his face.

"That's Dad's work friend, too. I met him once," Jake said.

"He's in all of the pictures."

Behind the glass door, in the middle of the cubicles, a man could be seen peeking his head out and over his cubicle and watching them. In each photo, he tilted his head this way and that, not taking his eyes off them for even a moment. In the shot Tillie had taken just before Jim walked away, the two men appeared to be looking directly at each other. Jim had his eyes shifted so far toward the back of the room that the picture only showed the whites of his eyes and a small sliver of brown, and the man in the back stared directly at him. No, he didn't stare. He glared. His pointer finger pressed against his lips, demanding silence. Tillie could almost hear a "Shhh" hissing out of the picture.

Jake looked from the camera to Tillie.

"They're hiding something," he said.

6

The Blue Chevy

THEIR PHONES RANG AT THE SAME TIME.

The camera dropped from Tillie's hand and swung down against her chest.

"Mom," Tillie said, turning her body at an angle away from Jake. She hadn't been paying close enough attention to the time.

"Mom!" Jake hollered into his phone. "I told you! I'll be home by— Oh." His voice quieted a little. "Mom, if the Wi-Fi isn't working, it's probably the router again."

"Why on earth are you still at school?" her mom demanded.

"Because it's the first meeting, and so there's, like, extra stuff to do," Tillie said, hearing the lie come out easily. "I'll be home soon."

As her mom began her list of health questions, Tillie mumbled, "I feel fine. I gotta go, though."

"Mom, I'll be home in a little bit and fix it then," Jake continued to his mom, scratching his head anxiously and releasing a bunch of dandruff. "Yeah, just finishing up at Art Club." He looked over at Tillie and winked. When he winked, his whole face scrunched up except one stretched-out eye. "I'll just walk home with some friends. I can stop and grab a sandwich for dinner or something. I'll be home in a while." Jake groaned. "I told you, I stopped with that graffiti stuff. It was stupid." He paused. "But even you have to admit that a Stop sign looks better with a smiley face on it."

From Tillie's free ear she heard what amounted to a squawk on the other end of the line.

"Sorry!" Jake said. "Okay, fine, I'll head home and fix the computer."

He hung up. Tillie was still listening to her mom go through the whole host of problems that could inflame her nerves if she overexerted herself and how it was terrible of the school to keep students so late, Art Club or not, and when would Tillie be home, and on and on.

"She's freaking out. Probably because my dad was always the guy who fixed the little stuff," Jake said to Tillie as she gave him a "Be quiet!" look. But he was really talking to himself, like a stand-up comedian playing to an empty room. Jake kicked some pebbles with his toes, watching them scatter from the sidewalk onto the grass. "And also she probably needs the computer to help her figure out stuff about my dad . . . I'm thinking she definitely knows something, and is probably just doing what we're doing. Trying to figure out how to help him, right? Not like I'd ever know what my mom really feels about anything. She's, like, *inscrutable*." He continued talking, mostly to his feet, ignoring that Tillie was still on the phone.

The other end of the phone line shifted from a monologue to ominous silence. Her mom had heard Jake's voice, and Tillie's lateness had become the last of her priorities.

"Mom, it's just a kid in the club," Tillie said quickly.

"It's the boy from the phone, isn't it?" her mom grilled her.

How did moms know everything?

"No, I'm out in the hallway because you called and interrupted!" Tillie lied. She gave Jake a look of murder and put a finger to her lip, shushing him—just like the cubicle man had shushed Jim, she realized with a shiver.

65

"Honey, are you really at Art Club? Are you being honest with me?"

"Mom!" she answered a little too harshly, and immediately felt bad. She *was* lying, after all. "Mom, yes, I swear I'm at Art Club. With Ms. Martinez, remember?" she added. Her mom knew all about Ms. Martinez. "I'm just heading home now."

"Okay, I'll come pick you up. Leaving now."

"You don't have to pick me up. You don't! I'm going to take the bus and take a few pictures on my way. Of . . . squirrels," she said, her voice slowing and slipping to a wisp.

"Come now, honey. Come right home. No excuses. You'll tire yourself out," her mom warned.

"Okay. Bye."

"Oops," Jake said when it was clear Tillie had gotten into some trouble. "I didn't mean to be so loud. She'll still buy it, right? We can keep looking now? Real quick?"

"I've got to go," Tillie grumbled. "Maple Street will have to wait. Besides, my leg . . ."—she almost stopped, but instead let the words spill out—"is probably going to start hurting really badly soon. It always does after a lot of walking. And my mom can always tell if it's hurting

66

by the sound of my voice. Then she tells Dad and he gets all . . . I can't . . . do stuff. Like this."

Maybe that was why she never spoke to other kids, because people might hear everything in her voice. They might hear that she could only walk just so much farther, for just so much longer. They might hear the part of her that wanted to stand on chairs and decorate the classroom for Thanksgiving, but instead had to sit and staple the tail feathers to the paper turkeys; the part of her that wrote essays on personal health and the history of athletics during gym class and hated it; and the part of her that headed to the bus every single day after school instead of staying to watch a school basketball game or rehearse for the school play, because if she didn't, the next day her body would be tired and so her muscles would get more tight and her leg would be even more feeble for a few days and her mom wouldn't let her go out and take pictures.

"I can't," she repeated.

Jake stopped. "Okay," he answered, as if she had said something totally normal. "Flagpole tomorrow, then?"

"I can't claim 'Art Club' two days in a row. Plus, I have stuff." A doctor's appointment. A collage project to work on for Ms. Martinez. And then there was the fact that the guy in the cubicle scared her a little. "Gotta go," she said.

"Let me carry the camera and your bag to the bus for you," Jake offered.

Her leg, indeed, had just started to ache terribly. "Okay," she relented, sighing.

Not looking directly at him, she handed Jake her bag. They walked in silence to the town bus.

✳   ✳   ✳

When they arrived at the empty bus stop, Tillie took a seat and Jake put her bag down by her feet.

"Okay. We'll talk soon, then." He took a step away. "If anything happens, I'll call you."

Tillie nodded, put a hand up to signal her goodbye, and looked down at her camera, clicking through the pictures.

"'Kay, bye," she heard him say.

Mere seconds later, she felt a smack on her arm. "What the—"

Jake stood next to her again, nearly jumping up and down. "Tillie! Tillie, that's the car!" he shouted.

She looked up and saw a blue car driving slowly toward them on the largely traffic-free road.

"The blue Chevy! I swear to God, it's following me!" Jake bolted out into the street.

"Wait!" Tillie yelled. "Careful!"

But there was no stopping him.

"Get pictures!" he hollered back as he hurtled toward the vehicle.

Tillie hopped up and stood at the curb, taking dozens of photos as the car neared Jake. It slowed down as it came closer and closer, though it was still too far to quite make out a face. A glare from the sun blocked any view through the windshield, though Tillie thought she may have seen the silhouette of a baseball cap.

The car made a sudden U-turn and sped off.

Why would it do that? Why wouldn't the driver just honk and tell the dumb kid to get out of his way?

Jake stood there, in the middle of the road, waving his hands. "Aw, come on!" he bellowed. "Come back, coward!"

"Jake, get out of the street!" Tillie felt like her mom as she imagined him getting hurt, a driver coming too fast, not seeing him. "*Get out!*" Her voice cracked. She closed her eyes for a moment, opening them to see Jake trotting back toward her and the bus coming down the road.

He arrived by her side, out of breath, just in time to

say, "I told you. Something weird is going on. Do you believe me?"

"I believe you," Tillie answered as the bus doors opened. "You were right." And she got on.

When Tillie arrived home, her mom put on a smile like everything was fine and asked, "So, how was it?"

"Really good," Tillie gushed as convincingly as she could, and to get out of any further interrogation she said, "Gotta study. So much history homework. Mind if I eat dinner in my room tonight?"

Avoiding her mom's face in case her eyes had questions in them, Tillie was already turning away as she heard her mom agree.

But later that night, as Tillie headed down the hall to brush her teeth, she heard low voices through her parents' door. She stopped in front of their room and listened.

"Will you give it a rest?" her dad said, his volume peaking before her mother's "Shhh!" silenced him.

Tillie, a well-practiced expert in avoiding the squeaks of the hardwood hallway floor, tiptoed back to her room to grab her camera.

Taking pictures through a keyhole was easier than one might think. Tillie had done some reading about old photography in art class, and knew that the first camera ever invented was a box with a tiny peephole in it, capturing images of light onto metal plates coated with a chemical called bitumen and then made visible by lavender oil. Considering all that, it was simple to look through the old-timey keyhole in her parents' bedroom door and take photos. Returning to their door, Tillie crouched down in front of her personal spyhole.

"She's got a boyfriend, someone she's spending time with," her mom rasped. "And you don't care."

Tillie snapped a blurred, half-dark picture of her mother pulling off her socks and throwing them into the hamper.

"No, she doesn't, Laura." Her dad sat still on the bed, his head in his hands.

"Yes, she does! She quite clearly does!"

Her dad sighed and looked up toward her mom, who was now throwing every item of clothing she saw into the hamper, dirty or no. "And how would that happen, Laura? She's . . ." He paused and looked toward the door.

Tillie held her breath and didn't blink, didn't snap a shot.

He turned back and Tillie exhaled, capturing his profile. "She's a *twelve-year-old with disabilities*," he whispered. "Come on, she doesn't have a boyfriend."

Tillie's stomach flip-flopped and she felt a stab of pain in her hip as if her dad's words had landed there.

Tillie's mother stopped in her tracks. "And so what, Andy? What does that have to do with anything?" her mom said. Whenever they argued they tended to call each other by their first names, instead of their usual "honey" or "love."

Thanks, Mom, Tillie thought.

"Nothing! *Nothing!* I just—" her dad sputtered.

"And she's almost *thirteen*. Which you'd see if you ever really looked at her," her mom spat out. "You never *look at her*."

The veins on her mom's face and neck nearly tore out of her skin.

"I *do* look at her, Laura!" her dad spat back. "I try! I— You know how I feel about her, okay? But," he went on with a choked voice, "you know I hate to drive her places. You know I can't . . ."

"Stand it. I know. I've heard."

They were stock-still, looking at each other for a moment.

"It's been over four years," her mom said. "*Four years*."

She paused. "Andy, I want *you* to take her to the doctor's tomorrow," she commanded. "*You'll* pick her up from school. And *you'll* talk to her about that boy."

Tillie slid back toward her room before she could hear her dad refuse. She was certain she would get a voicemail from him the next day saying he couldn't make it, because she already knew that, to her dad, four years was like no time at all.

7

Blind Artist

TILLIE WAITED ON THE BENCH AT THE BUS STOP by school. Her knees started to shiver and bump each other a bit. She pulled her jacket tighter and crossed her arms to combat the chill of the March day. In Illinois, spring took its time. Sometimes it wasn't warm until May.

Charlie Jordan walked by her on his way home, his face buried in a book, as usual, but somehow he managed to navigate the sidewalk in a straight line. Cara Dale and Lily James followed a few minutes behind him, giggling together, Lily acting out some moment from the day.

A small brown car with a multicolored beaded rosary

hanging from the rearview mirror pulled up to the curb. When the window rolled down, Tillie saw it was Ms. Martinez, on her way home from school. Ms. Martinez gave her a big smile.

"Hey there! How's the collage going?" Ms. Martinez asked her with a friendly wink.

"Well," Tillie said, "I miscalculated the size of the corner images, so they ended up being too large. They overwhelm the whole thing. It's my fault. I planned the sizes of the images wrong. I need to start over." Tillie blushed. That was a lot of information for a simple question.

"We all make mistakes," Ms. Martinez said to Tillie from the driver's seat through her open car window. "And not only do mistakes happen to everybody," Ms. Martinez continued, "but mistakes can be a good thing."

Tillie looked at her like she was out of her mind, and Ms. Martinez laughed.

"Really! A big part of being a good artist is making a mistake, and then figuring out how to use that to make the piece even better." A couple of cars drove by, parents and kids leaving the school parking lot, but Ms. Martinez stayed right there, parked by the curbside, talking to her. "My watercolor teacher in college called it a 'happy accident.' So don't worry about starting your collage all over again, just make the awkwardness of the corners do something different for the whole thing. Maybe make it a collage that celebrates awkwardness."

Tillie sighed. She pulled her coat around herself tighter. "But I miscalculated all the shapes of the pictures," she said. "The whole thing looks too . . . *blah*. Nothing catches the eye, like you said it should."

Ms. Martinez smiled. One tooth in her smile jutted out slightly. "I'll be the judge of that."

Ms. Martinez turned her head away from Tillie and looked up and down the road. She twisted her torso to glance toward the school parking lot and then back at Tillie.

"Is someone picking you up, Tillie?" Her smile faded. Her voice softened. "It's pretty chilly out here."

Tillie mimicked Ms. Martinez's looks up and down the road, as if she were expecting someone. She felt her face flush pink. Her dad's voicemail replayed in her head: *Hey, Til. I'm so sorry, but I'm overloaded at work. I know it's not ideal, but you're going to have to take the town bus today, okay? I'm . . . I'm sorry. See you in a bit. Nachos later? Or something? Okay. Bye.* "I'm just waiting for the bus," she said, moving her eyes toward her feet. Typically, she'd call her mom in this kind of situation, but she just didn't want to hear a bunch of excuses about her dad.

"Oh, okay," Ms. Martinez said, nodding. "But what about the school bus?"

Another car drove by, this one with some of Tillie's classmates in it, and they waved at Ms. Martinez. She waved back, with a momentary flash of a smile, and then focused her gaze on Tillie again.

Tillie paused and then told her, "Well, my dad got held up at work and I have a doctor's appointment. The school bus doesn't go as near to there as the town bus. I'm not sick or anything," she added, feeling stupid.

Ms. Martinez just nodded again. A slow, thoughtful nod. "Well, why don't you come hitch a ride with me?"

Tillie's head automatically shook in a "No." "I can't do that, Ms. Martinez," Tillie said. "I'm fine. I'm totally okay. I do this all the time."

As she said the words, she saw Ms. Martinez unlock her side of the door.

"Hop in." She smiled. "Come on."

Tillie put her hands on her shaking knees and pushed herself up. Holding her head high and her abdomen tight in an effort to make her limp appear as minimal as possible, she walked the few steps to Ms. Martinez's car. Right as they pulled away, the bus came.

"It's much better in here, don't you think?" Ms. Martinez said as they headed off.

Tillie relaxed into the seat and watched the streets around them wind along. She lifted her camera to take a couple of shots of town through the window.

She felt her phone buzz in her coat pocket. Tillie eyed the text from Jake. He'd told her at lunch that he hadn't seen the car this morning, but there'd been a couple of calls and hang-ups from the blocked number the night before.

no sign of the blue chevy after school either . . .
we scared it off i guess

K. Talk soon, Tillie wrote back.

"Where to?" Ms. Martinez asked.

What if Tillie told her it was a hundred miles away? Could she stay in Ms. Martinez's car the rest of the day?

"It's downtown. Off Main Street, near the high school."

"Oh, perfect. That's right near my house! Mind if I turn on some music?"

Ms. Martinez began to hum along to her radio. The lyrics said something about cities and pretty girls and guitars. The singer managed to sound whiny and romantic at the same time. "Do you know this song?" Ms. Martinez asked her.

"No," Tillie answered.

"Makes me think of New York," Ms. Martinez said as they took a left.

"I've never been."

"No? I think you'd like it. There are a million things you could photograph. On every street."

"Really?"

"Oh, yeah." Ms. Martinez grinned.

"So you've been there on trips?"

"I lived there, actually," she said.

"Really?" Tillie asked. "Aren't you from here, though? Someone can go from *this* place to New York City?"

"I went to high school here, yeah. But then I went to art school in New York."

Tillie knew many things about Ms. Martinez because she worked on projects in Ms. Martinez's classroom at lunchtime once a week. Sometimes Ms. Martinez would talk about herself. Tillie had learned that she wasn't married, she loved to draw with coal pencils, she thought George Clooney was the handsomest movie star of all time, and she wrote letters to Illinois politicians requesting more funding for art programs in public schools and thought that all the students should, too. Tillie had learned, in other words, that Ms. Martinez was amazing. But Tillie hadn't heard about New York.

"I went there to paint," Ms. Martinez told her, keeping an eye on the road, but every now and then tilting her chin toward Tillie. "I *wanted* to paint, rather, but actually—somewhat randomly—one of my teachers suggested a sculpture piece I did to this art curator he knew, and they put it in an art show. So people started to think of me as a sculptor."

"That's awesome!"

"It was okay." Ms. Martinez shrugged, and her eyes looked like they were far away somewhere. "I actually used to have an art stand on a small street in the city. I sold miniature sculptures there. Of women dancing. I called them my 'little women.'"

Tillie wanted to take a picture of Ms. Martinez right then so badly. But instead she listened.

"But I wasn't really a sculptor. Or a New Yorker, I suppose. So I came back. I really wanted to be a teacher." She paused, and her eyes returned from far away. Her voice brightened. "And now I have my wonderful students, like you!" She moved in toward Tillie with her shoulder as if to nudge her, though they didn't touch.

"Wow," Tillie marveled. "If I had an art stand in New York, I would never leave."

They whirled past Lake Avenue, and the thought of Jake and the lost father and the man in the cubicle hit Tillie.

"I think you can definitely make it to New York, if you want to," Ms. Martinez said. "Your photographs are beautiful."

With those words, Jake's dad evaporated from her thoughts. Tillie must have looked shocked, because Ms. Martinez laughed and said, "Really, Tillie! Art should capture something true, you know? And your photos do that."

It was the first time anyone had called her photography "art."

They were on Main Street now, moments away from Dr. Kregger's.

Ms. Martinez paused, squinting and leaning her head toward the windshield. "So what street are we looking for?" she asked. Even in such an awkward position, Tillie saw, Ms. Martinez was graceful. She had the neck of a ballerina, but a full and dimpled face. Her hair, consistently smoothed back into a sleek ponytail, was a pure black.

"It's on Thompson Street. The corner," Tillie told her regretfully. She didn't want to leave the car.

"Ah, okay. Sorry, I can't find my glasses—I lost them last week—so the letters are a little blurry. I'm wearing an old pair with my old prescription. They're so funny-looking, right? Huge. I call them my 'grandma glasses.'"

Maybe teachers could use the Lost and Found, too. And, like Jake had said, she really could find anything. So with a little bravery, Tillie said, "I could help you find them, maybe. If you want. Did you lose them at school?"

"I think so," Ms. Martinez said. "I feel like I last had them there. But don't worry about it, Tillie. Just make me a great, mistake-filled photo collage."

She kept looking for street signs, squinting her eyes more and more, until she looked like a beautiful mole.

Tillie felt herself giggling. "Your eyesight is pretty bad, Ms. Martinez, huh?"

"Yup," she said. "I'm a blind artist."

"I'm sure the glasses are in pictures I took in your class. I can totally figure out where you left them. Maybe you put them down somewhere and I got a shot of it."

Ms. Martinez made a face of disapproval but couldn't hide a smile. "Oh, so you're taking pictures in my class, are you? I didn't know I was blind enough to miss that. I thought pictures were for out-of-class time."

"Yeah." Tillie smiled back. "Sorry . . ."

"Oh, hey, that's where I live, over there." Ms. Martinez nodded toward a little brick house with a small porch on a residential street right on the corner of Main Street and Clareview. They flew right by it, but not before Tillie lifted up her camera and in a flash took a picture of it through the car window.

"Not far from your doctor's, I guess." Then, laughing at herself, Ms. Martinez said, "I really need your help reading these street signs, Til."

"We're almost there, Ms. Martinez," Tillie said, feeling the happiest she'd felt in a while.

Tillie looked down at the shot she'd taken of Ms. Martinez's house. She tried to imagine Ms. Martinez sitting on the porch, maybe with a sketchbook in her hand, her hair out of the ponytail after her workday, the thick strands tucked behind her ears, waving at the kids who walked by. Maybe she had a shelf full of all her old "little women" sculptures. Tillie pictured the house at nighttime, a light on in the window, Ms. Martinez sitting on her couch watching George Clooney movies.

Thompson Street arrived and Tillie directed Ms. Martinez toward it. The sign above the tiny office, which was in an old house, read "Rehabilitation and Pain Management, Dr. Samuel Kregger, MD," the words written in bright blue letters surrounded by bubbly stars, making the place appear more homey than it actually was. Reluctant to leave, Tillie wished she didn't have to go to the doctor's appointment at all. In the office, she'd hear the same thing as always—"Everything's looking great, Tillie!"—which really meant, "You look exactly the same and things won't change, but here's some new medicine to help with the pain in the calf, and here's some for the inflammation of the nerves, and because of a random car accident, you won't be able to do a whole bunch of things ever again," and then she'd be on her way.

As Ms. Martinez pulled up to the curb, Tillie inhaled the scent of her car. It smelled like the two short weeks in May when lilacs bloom. It must've been her perfume.

Tillie took a deep breath to steel herself and asked, her voice a tad shaky, "Hey, Ms. Martinez? Would you mind if I took your portrait real quick?"

"Not at all, Tillie." As Ms. Martinez turned toward Tillie, she said, "They say a picture is worth a thousand words, right? Maybe your pictures can tell my story, huh?" Ms. Martinez smiled sweetly, her head tilted to the side. "How's that?"

"Perfect." Tillie beamed and took the shot. "Thanks for the ride," she said as she opened the door.

"No problem, Tillie. See you tomorrow. You and all your excellent mistakes."

8

Into the Night

WHEN TILLIE'S MOM PICKED HER UP AFTER THE appointment, she apologized over and over for her dad flaking out, and asked her a million questions about what the doctor said. The car smelled like worry and stress and the sweat of a long workday, without a whiff of lilacs or anything easy and flowery at all.

Back at home, in front of the full-length mirror in her closet, she held her film camera against her chest and took a photo of herself. Ms. Martinez was right—pictures told stories. Just like Ms. Martinez's told the story of an artist, and the man in the cubicle's told one of a secret, her picture told a story, too. But of what? A quiet girl with a limp? A detective, like Jake had said? What was *her* story?

On her laptop, Tillie zoomed in on the face of the man in the cubicle, cropping the shot into a blurry portrait. Cursing herself for having used her range finder on its automatic setting, sacrificing crispness and detail for expediency, she pressed print.

Tillie's aunt Kerry had given her a photo printer as a Hanukkah present one year, and it wasn't the highest quality, but it was a life-changer. Her mom often pleaded with her to cut down on printing. The price of ink and paper added up. Tillie tried to be choosy about what she printed, but sometimes it was hard to resist, and in the case of a mystery like this, it was nearly impossible.

She grabbed the warm, wet print of the cubicle man. Tillie couldn't make out the color of his eyes, but she could see that they were placed far back in his face. His eyebrows made a straight line. And was it just in her imagination, or did he have a scar? A small one, right above his left eye?

Tillie had to put the portrait away. If she didn't finish her Elizabeth Cady Stanton paper that night, she'd be in big trouble in history class. As long as she got a B she was fine, but a C or lower would be a problem and give her mom something else to worry about.

But this man's face pulled her in. His face, and Jim's jittery avoidance, and the car's U-turn . . . They added up to something.

His face provided her only clue. She'd almost caught the blue Chevy's license plate in one of her shots, but she couldn't make out the last digit. How could she decode the meaning behind the finger covering Cubicle Man's lips? What was he telling Jim to keep quiet about?

But it didn't need to be solved *tonight*, she told herself. It couldn't be. She had other work to do. And not just history class.

Diana Farr had given her an assignment: Find out if Joaquin Silva liked her as much as she thought he did. Ordinarily, Tillie wouldn't take on all these "personal" cases, but Diana was an exception to any rule. After all, Diana had basically created her.

"He's so cute, right? I always feel him looking at me," Diana had said to her. "I need to know if I'm right."

She was. After a quick scan through the "Lunchroom Photos" file on her laptop, Tillie found the admittedly cute Joaquin gawking at Diana in four different shots within only two weeks. In one, his chin rested on his palm, his eyes aimed at the back of Diana's perfectly highlighted head as she spoke animatedly to some other boy. In another, the camera caught him glancing her way as she strolled by with her tray. In still others, he beamed over toward her as she spoke at her lunch table, his swooning eyes nearly begging her to look back at him.

She'd tell Diana tomorrow.

She picked up her biography of Elizabeth Cady Stanton. But, putting it down, her fingers—as if they were magnetized—returned toward the Cubicle Man photo on her desk's corner.

What is Jake's mom's part in all this? Tillie thought as she gazed at the man's face. Jake figured his mom was protecting him from something, but what if she was just protecting herself? Maybe the bank statements were a part of something more nefarious. What if she had something to do with his dad's disappearance? What if she had . . . hurt him somehow? Maybe Zayde and Bubbe's money wasn't enough for her. Maybe she had something more in mind . . .

Tillie pushed the thought away and put the picture down. Yes, something was bizarre about Jake's dad. But they weren't in an action movie.

She turned to another case of hers.

Hailey Granito had lost a sheet of homework she'd

done and was freaking out because it was due the next Monday, and in a wide shot Tillie had taken of the classroom as she was leaving it, a folder lay visible under Hailey's desk. The paper was probably in it. It was most likely in the real lost and found in the office, or with the math teacher, who might have picked it up after class. Simple enough. Hailey lost things once a week.

Back to Cubicle Man.

He appeared to be bald, but maybe he had patches of hair in the back, where the camera's lens couldn't reach. His glasses reflected the dim light of a computer screen. He glowered at Jim with such focus that without knowing he was in a cubicle someone looking at the picture might have thought he was a Bond villain.

No, it couldn't be Jake's mom who was behind any of this lost-dad confusion. It all came down, in some way, to this man. This man, with his beady, menacing little face, and his finger, placed against his lips, sealing off something essential from her and Jake. Something that frightened her.

As crazy as Jake sometimes sounded, she saw that some kind of huge, grown-up secret just might exist here. And it couldn't be cracked as easily as determining if a gorgeous boy had a crush on a gorgeous girl. Jake had called it "the big, bad world." It was true she hadn't seen much of it, but maybe she didn't want to.

She shut off the questions in her mind, and forced out a history paper.

※　※　※

Tillie heard her dad come home from work, and she made her way down to the doorway where he was taking off his shoes and coat.

"Hey, Dad," she said, leaning against the wall.

"Oh, hey, Til," he replied with a pre-apology sigh. "I am so sorry I couldn't pick you up today. I really was overloaded at work and I—"

"It's okay." Tillie cut him off hurriedly. "Um, I'm curious about something. For school."

"Oh." He leaned against the wall opposite her. "Yeah, okay, sure."

"What's the most unbelievable story you ever worked on?"

He gave her a quizzical look. "I . . ." He hesitated.

"I mean . . ." She paused to collect her thoughts. "Have you ever worked on a story where some normal person was caught up in an out-of-the-movies-type situation? Like, does anything in the movies, or anything even like that, ever actually happen?"

"What class is this for?"

"History," she answered too hastily.

"Hmm." Her dad's face lit up a little. "I guess the one thing that comes to mind is a story I worked on, back when I was a student, actually, about people who find out they've been married for years to spies. You know, you don't know your husband or wife is in the CIA or something, or even—back in the eighties, especially—some people were married to foreign spies without knowing."

"*What?*" Tillie's jaw fell. "And they didn't *know* it?"

"Yeah! It ruins people's lives. They'll live for years, decades sometimes, not knowing."

Tillie tried to process all this. "Okay, well, what about things like people going on the run, or getting kidnapped or blackmailed or something?" It seemed just as unimaginable as marriage to a spy.

"One thing you learn very quickly working in the news is that life can be a lot more unbelievable than you ever thought." He shrugged, as if embarrassed at his own passion on the topic. "But I, personally, have not worked on any kidnapping cases."

"Okay," Tillie said, nodding. "Okay, Dad. Great. Thanks!"

She left her dad in the hallway and headed to her room to text Jake.

I got the license plate but it's too fuzzy to make out all of it. We need to focus on Cubicle Man.

Jake responded, **next stop—house on maple street**

Tillie pulled out her laptop and started watching one of her parents' favorite shows she hadn't started yet—a British mystery.

Twenty minutes into it, her parents' voices infiltrated the story.

She turned off the show and the lights and put a pillow over her head. She knew who the murderer was, anyway. It was always so obvious.

Tillie fell asleep to her mom's voice.

I can't believe you didn't pick her up from school. What is wrong with you?

She dreamt of finding the ginger-haired, happy-looking man, leading him to Jake and watching them embrace, both of them thanking her for saving him from the evil Cubicle Man.

✳   ✳   ✳

Her cell phone rang at two in the morning. Tillie jumped up.

"*Hello?*" she answered, knowing who it was within a groggy split second. "Why are you calling?"

"Because I needed to reach you," the whispering voice responded.

Tillie sighed a sleepy sigh.

"I thought we could go to Maple Street. You couldn't go earlier."

Tillie pulled herself up to sit. She felt her leg twitch like it always did upon waking and she stretched her back so that it would wake up with her. She looked out the window and saw the glow of the street lamps. There was no moon tonight.

"I'm sleeping."

"Not anymore, you aren't." She could hear Jake's pleased-with-himself smile through the phone line.

"You're out of your mind."

"I know."

"Good night, Jake."

"Wait!" Jake's whisper shifted to a raspy plea. "You know we have to find him. You saw those guys being so weird. Like, who's afraid of two twelve-year-olds? You saw the car. You said you'd go with me."

"I told you I was busy today."

"But now it's tomorrow."

Tillie groaned.

"Look, he's either detained somewhere, by someone, or he's running and hiding from someone or something. And I think that if he wanted to send me a message, or leave a clue for me, he'd leave it in the tree house at the old house."

"Even if I wanted to go, Jake," she said, feeling herself become more awake, "it's nighttime. That's . . . dangerous." She sounded more like her mom than she would have liked.

Jake laughed quietly. "Oh, yeah, because of all the crime in Templeton. Murder and mayhem."

He was right. The only crimes that ever happened in their town were probably the noise violations from the college's one fraternity.

"Besides," he continued, "I've snuck out lots before. One time my dad even caught me, and he wasn't so mad. He just sighed and was like, 'You're a rabble-rouser, kid.' Come on, Tillie. Have a little adventure! Live a little! Rabble-rouse with me!"

"Well, how would we even *get* to Maple Street? The buses don't run past midnight and it's a long walk."

"It's like fifteen minutes from your house," Jake said. "I'll pick you up."

"In a car? Wow, you're pretty small for a sixteen-year-old," Tillie responded. Jake turned her into a teasing, sarcastic person she felt like she had never met before.

"Ha-ha," Jake fake-laughed. "I mean I'll—what's the word?—*escort* you."

"It doesn't take *me* fifteen minutes to walk," she said with an anger in her voice that surprised her. "It takes me double. Maybe more than double. If you haven't noticed, I walk kind of slowly."

"You're right." Jake paused. "I'll have to do something about that."

"You would be way ahead of people with medical degrees, then," Tillie scoffed.

"Never underestimate me, Tillie. My great-grandpa was a doctor."

Tillie got out of her bed and put her ear to her door. There was no sound. The house was asleep.

Meanwhile Jake was going on and on about an old movie he'd seen with his dad called *North by Northwest*, in which some random guy is on the run because the wrong people think he's a spy.

"A spy?" Tillie heard herself ask.

"The point is, the guy had to run away," Jake explained. He proceeded to tell her the entire plot of the film.

Tillie went to her pictures and poured them out of their folder onto the desk again. She picked up the picture of the cubicle man and held it under the light by the window. She shuddered.

"Jake, I can't go out," she said as he finished the story.

"I already have a plan. I'll be there in twenty minutes. You'll walk just fine."

"Jake!" Tillie protested. "What if I get caught? What if something happens and I can't get back? I don't do this stuff. I don't talk at two in the morning. And I don't sneak out!"

"Well, maybe it's about time you start doing some more things! You can do it," Jake assured her. "Just don't get caught. I'll see you in twenty minutes, outside your house."

"I don't even know *how* to sneak out," she said.

"How do you normally leave your house?"

"I . . . walk out the door? Obviously."

"Try that." He hung up.

Tillie paced by the window. Five minutes went by. She texted him.

You better not be coming over here.

There was no response.

Hellooooo. This was not the deal.

I WORK ALONE. I told you.

Nothing.

Tillie's heart pounded. Sometimes, when she was about to embark on a long day, she could feel her heart beat in her feet, and sometimes she could feel it when she saw something that she knew would make a perfect photograph. She tried to wiggle her toes to get the pulsing, thrilling, painful feeling out of her appendages.

She put on her hoodie and grabbed her DSLR. "Live a little," she whispered to herself. She kept her pajama pants on, figuring that if her parents saw her walking out she could make up a lie more easily than if she had jeans on. The PJs had moons and hearts on them, and Jake would see them. Her eleven-year-old self had picked them out at Target and destined her twelve-year-old self for embarrassment. She stopped for a second in the hallway and considered going back to change, but then she decided she didn't care.

The silence Tillie had learned from sneaking snapshots of her parents got her through the hallway and out the door without a sound.

She sat on the steps and waited quietly for Jake. So much time went by that she started to think of one of those movies where a girl gets stood up for prom. Sometimes the girl never got over it. Sometimes they showed the character years later, still thinking about it, still never having been kissed. But, ew, she didn't want to be kissed by Jake.

As Tillie's eyes began to droop and close, Jake showed up.

"Hey, there!"

"Shhh," Tillie responded. Her parents' window was literally a stone's throw away.

Jake rolled his eyes.

He wore a flashlight tied with a thick string around his neck and carried a long black bag. Tillie noticed that it, too, had a moon design on it. She fingered the sides of her pajama pants.

"What's that?" she asked.

"Oh, just equipment. You have a camera? Of course you do. Okay." Jake gave his scalp a big scratch.

Tillie's foot throbbed a little more intensely. "So how am I going to do this?" she whispered. "It'll take me forever to walk that far."

"Never fear," Jake declared.

He dug into his bag, which reached all the way down to his feet, and pulled out a long, straight branch with some kind of carving on one end.

"And what. Is that."

"It's Gandalf's walking stick!"

"It's what?"

"A walking stick."

"I heard you."

"I was Gandalf for Halloween," Jake told her. "This is

his walking stick, or his walking stick-slash-wand, I guess you'd say. Is that the right word? He also has a sword, but the costume didn't come with that, so . . . sorry."

"No. Absolutely not using a staff."

"His *staff*! That's the word. Tillie, what knowledge of the wonderful world of fantasy have you been hiding from me? And come *on*," he said, dragging out the "on" like a little kid, "it's perfect."

"No, I am not walking with that," Tillie declared, and she stood up. She would look ridiculous with a big wizard staff from Halloween.

A couple of cats chased each other through her yard and she jumped, knocking herself off balance a little. Jake grabbed her arm as she steadied herself and moved to reach for the doorknob.

"Wait. I knew you'd be embarrassed."

"I am not embarrassed, it just won't help!" What embarrassed her was being told she was embarrassed.

"So look." Jake reached into his bag again. "Look what else I brought," he said as he searched around in what she now realized was some kind of wizard bag. With an expression of triumph, Jake pulled out a huge mass of what looked like gray fur.

"And what is *that*?" Tillie turned back from the doorknob. "A puppy?"

"It's Gandalf's beard. If I wear it, we can both be wizardy-looking together."

Jake stretched the beard's elastic band, pulled it over his head, and set the long gray beard in place.

He looked like a young boy with an aging disease.

Tillie began to laugh. With her first burst of laughter, Jake hushed her, though he was starting to snicker, too. Tillie quieted herself, her shoulders still bouncing from giggles. But then she laughed again. A loud laugh, one that was so enormous she moved away from the step on her doorway and toward the sidewalk, doubling over. She laughed so hard that when she took the walking stick and started to use it, it shook a little beneath her hands even as it steadied her.

"I'm glad you like my idea," Jake said, beaming.

And together, young but old, hobbling but moving toward balance, the two detective-wizards headed down the sidewalk and embarked into the night.

9

Old Man at the Window

SHE REALLY DID WALK BETTER WITH GANDALF'S staff. Maybe it was time to reconsider her use of the cane packed away, abandoned, in her mom's closet. People had stared at her a lot more back when she'd used it.

But there was no one to stare at her tonight on the empty streets.

"Hello, old friend," Jake said softly as they arrived at 308 Maple Street.

"Wow," Tillie marveled. She had seen the house in the family album Jake had shown her, but in person it loomed above them. Maybe Jake's dad's old job was a better one. In their town, a lot of people's parents seemed to have less-good jobs the past couple of years. The night cloaked the white house in a grayish blue. The house had a real porch, not a tiny step holding a single metal chair like at Tillie's.

Someone had taped a painting of stick figures on the inside of the front door's window.

"You're not worried about waking anybody up?" Tillie asked.

Jake didn't respond. She turned to see him still gazing at the house, a dreamy look in his eye. Then, after a few seconds, he spoke.

"That's why we're here at night. We'll just sneak into the backyard where the tree house is and be quiet."

"Okay . . ."

"Hey, I know you're a lot smarter than me, but give me a little credit here, Hermione."

"You and the wizard references," Tillie mumbled.

"Hermione's a witch, actually . . ."

Tillie shushed him.

"For not having any siblings, we're both surprisingly good at bantering," he said, turning to her for the first time since they'd arrived. "I'm proud of us."

"No one uses the word 'bantering.' That beard really is making you old," Tillie said under her breath, unable to hide a grin. "You sound even more like my grandpa than usual."

"See? You're bantering again." Jake headed for the

fence and motioned for her to come along. "This fence is new. Really trying to keep out the riffraff, huh? Well, I guess we'll have to climb it," he said. "Let me think . . . Okay, you'll use Gandalf's staff to steady yourself, and I'll climb on your shoulders. Wait. Bad idea. Okay, okay, I got it. I'll dig a hole underneath the fence, and I'll go under, and you make your body go limp, and I'll pull you through."

Tillie pushed gently on the gate. It opened.

"Or we could do that," Jake said, following her in.

For such an expensive-looking house, it revealed a pretty bare backyard.

Tillie spotted a swing on a thick-trunked tree with tall, curving branches, and a rain-worn tree house propped up on the thinner tree next to it. It had small strips of wood peeling off it. There was a tiny hole carved in the front of it, probably for little-kid Jake to look out of to see when his parents were coming so he could stop his mischief, Tillie thought. A ladder led up to the box-in-the-sky, and it appeared rather precarious.

Tillie shivered and took a photo. She turned the flash off, to keep them disguised by the darkness. She'd grabbed her fastest lens, but still, most of these shots probably wouldn't turn out.

"Okay, we have to go up there," Jake said. "Come on."

It was Tillie's turn to sound harsher than usual. "I can't climb that!" She stepped away from him a little bit, using her walking stick to keep her balance in the cold mud of the backyard.

"Look, I know that if he couldn't talk to me or something, but wanted to send me some kind of message, there's a possibility he'd leave it up there. Some sign he was okay."

"Jake, it's not . . . realistic," Tillie said.

"Or maybe he's just been there and I'll find evidence of that. Evidence he's hiding from something. Trust me, if he's running or hiding from . . . *whatever*, then he's been here."

Cubicle Man's face emerged in Tillie's mind once again, hovering there like a ghost. She would hide from him, too, if he were after her.

"He was so happy in this house." Jake looked dreamy again, and a little sad. "We used to . . ." Jake paused, and took a breath, holding on to it for a little too long and then pouring it out in a stream of stories. "We built this together," he said, nodding up toward the tree house. "We used to hang out in it constantly. We read through all of Tolkien here on weekend afternoons. He's a Tolkien *fanatic*. He painted an awesome picture of Aragorn that's hanging in my room! And he taught me birdcalls. We played superheroes together. That's why I wore that red—well, pink—cape. He was Super Hawk and I was . . . I was Super Ladybug." Jake chuckled softly, and Tillie did, too. She could absolutely see fourth-grade Jake as a Super Ladybug type of kid. "I don't really remember why, but ladybugs *are* awesome, and totally underrated . . . Anyway," he said, his voice wistful, the night breeze blowing through his Gandalf beard, "when I wore the cape to school and people made fun of me, my dad was like, 'Listen, Super Ladybug, there will always be jerks around. Terrible jerks. Be a nice guy and have fun and enjoy being the guy you are and the jerks will just be a "blah blah blah" in your ear.' And I did what he said. I wore that cape every day for a year, and I loved it, and it was, like, the best year ever. So, thanks, Dad. And that's the magic of this tree house, okay? Anyone who had to hide would want to hide here. And he'd leave something behind for me. I know it."

Tillie tried to imagine her own dad talking to her like that and she couldn't. She thought of when Jake had made fun of her in sixth grade, and how *he* had been the "blah blah blah" in *her* ear.

His dad sounded really fun.

"Well, you'll have to search for evidence yourself." She considered handing him the camera, but felt her body resisting that idea as she clutched it tighter and pulled it against her chest.

"Tillie, give me a break, I need you!" He turned to her with his big eyes, surrounded by furry gray.

She stared up at the tree house. Sneaking out was enough. It was already too much. All of this. But climbing up a ladder? She'd break her bones again. Her other leg wouldn't work.

"I can't," she said. "I'll fall."

And that was that.

"Okay." Jake's eyes morphed from gloomy to determined. "I'm goin' up."

While Jake climbed the ladder, Tillie wandered toward the side of the house to the area right in front of where the fence began. Ivy grew on the walls and curled around a first-floor window like hair around a face. She wanted to capture the image so badly, but she had no light. She didn't want to ruin the night's shadow effects or wash out the cool colors that came from the slight glow of the neighbors' back porch lights, so she diffused the light of the flash by placing a hand in front of it. The light filled up her eyes and for a moment she was blinded, and then, once again, darkness surrounded her.

Out of that darkness, and the slightly open fence,

came Jake. His shoulders slouched. His beard sagged a little off his chin and a twig jutted out of the gray.

Tillie's hip and leg began to tremble a bit, and she sat down by the window.

"There's nothing up there," Jake grumbled, kicking the dirt. "This was stupid." He came toward Tillie and leaned against the outside of the house.

And then came a noise—a shuffling.

Tillie motioned for Jake to be quiet. She forced herself up. "What was that?" she whispered. Something was moving nearby, outdoors. Tillie began to tremble as she pictured Cubicle Man, his figure coming toward them in the dark, having followed them all the way there, stopping them from telling some secret they shouldn't know, keeping them from their search for answers.

"Jake . . ." she whispered, reaching for his arm.

And then they heard a scraping, like the sound of long nails against a door.

"What was that?" Jake said.

Tillie stopped breathing.

"It's him," Jake whispered. He hopped up and down. "It's him! He's here somewhere. He heard me. We found him."

"Or a different him . . ." Tillie whispered. "I can't run!" A shot of panic crept up her spine.

The scratching and shuffling seemed to get louder, but Tillie couldn't be sure.

"Wait," she said, so quietly she was really just mouthing words. "The noise is next to us."

Jake turned toward the fence to go back, but Tillie stopped him.

"It's not going to be your dad, Jake," Tillie said, holding his arm. "You know that."

They both stayed put. Silent, listening.

Tillie's eyes still pulsed a little from the flash. She squinted at their surroundings, studying, searching for what monsters prowled, and as she registered the strong breeze, and the foliage running along the house, she felt her whole body relax. There, right next to the window, she saw a leafless bush scraping along the outside of the house in a fury.

But Jake had already put his bearded face to the ivy-adorned first-floor window.

"I hear it in there," Jake said. "Hey, what if the people actually moved out, and my dad is hiding out in *there*?"

"No, Jake, it's just next to us. Look—" Tillie pointed to the bush, but Jake remained in another world.

His nose touching the glass, he spoke at full volume, "Dad? *Dad?*" Tillie tried to stop him, but he knocked on the window. "Dad!" he called out much too loudly.

And at that, a light switched on, the curtains opened, and a face appeared.

"Aaaaah!" screeched a little girl, her head peeking just above the windowsill, face-to-face with young Gandalf. *"Aaaaah!"*

"Aaaaah!" Jake screamed back, at almost the same piercing pitch.

As Jake and the girl both shrieked, Tillie snapped a shot, and then grabbed Jake's arm and pulled him away, leaving the little girl yelling for her parents.

"Dad, there's an old man at the window!" they heard as they hurried away into the empty streets, laughing even harder than two hours before, laughing so hard that Tillie saw the shimmers of tears in Jake's beard.

10

Bitten-Down Nails

MORNING CAME AND JAKE WAS RIGHT. NO ONE knew. Tillie was a girl who had snuck out of her house to solve a mystery. When she woke up from her two hours of sleep she took a picture of her own face.

Maybe she really could be a detective someday. Maybe she could even work for the CIA. Or maybe she could be a photojournalist who traveled around the world documenting wars. Maybe she could follow bands around the country and have her photographs in *Rolling Stone*. The world looked different. Anything seemed possible—everything.

Tillie brushed her hair that morning in front of the mirror, luxuriating in its length like a movie star. Then she put her glasses on, gave one last glance at her imperfect photo collage, placed her camera around her neck, and turned back into someone a little more like Tillie. She went to the kitchen before her mom had even called her to come.

On her way there she saw that she had received a text from Jake:

how many wizards does it take to change a lightbulb? none. wizards dont need lightbulbs! ha. one of my dads favorite jokes. c u in a couple hours!

She smiled and responded: **Witty. See you later, Super Ladybug.**

At the breakfast table her mom typed away on her laptop between bites of cereal, and her dad drank his coffee by the window above the sink, watching the bird feeder.

Tillie buzzed high on no sleep, excited for the day.

"Hey, guys," Tillie said to them, in a voice as chirpy as Jake's. Her mom looked up at her. It was only 7 a.m. and her face was already creased with what's-going-on-with-Tillie concern.

"Say 'cheese'!" Tillie took a picture with the flash on and light filled the room. "What are the birds up to, Dad?"

Tillie's dad blinked. "I wish you'd take a break with

that thing for a while. It's so early." He coughed, and mumbled something to himself, and went to sit at the kitchen table. "You used to love to feed the birds out there, remember?" he said, his head tilted downward, as if he were really speaking only to himself. "We'd bring the birdseed by the feeder. They sat in our hands." He picked up the newspaper and began to read.

Tillie stared at him. A break? From photographs?

Tillie heard Ms. Martinez's voice from the other day in her head. *Your pictures are beautiful.*

So she said, "Say 'cheese' again!"

Her dad covered his eyes with a hand.

"I sometimes don't know why Dad ever got her into this Vivian Maier stuff," he said to Tillie's mom, as if Tillie weren't there. He rubbed his stubbly cheek and yawned.

But Tillie *was* there. And she *was* into this stuff.

"Who's Vivian Maier?" she asked.

Her mom gave her a "No idea" look.

Tillie paused. She stopped her flashing, but she kept her camera in front of her face like a mask, peering through the viewfinder, first at her mom's almost-terrified-with-worry expression and then at her dad's annoyed one, and she pointed the lens there. *You're right,*

Dad, Tillie thought. *Grandpa should have gotten me into gymnastics instead. If only things had been different, huh?*

From behind the lens blocking her flushed face, Tillie said, "Never mind, Dad. You never look at my photos, anyway. So whatever." She took another picture of her dad's befuddled expression, let her camera fall against her chest, grabbed a piece of toast off the counter and added, "I'm off."

Her mom started to say something in response, but Tillie had already turned away toward the door.

At school, Tillie reported the good news about Joaquin to a delighted Diana Farr, who wanted to know the details of each recorded stare; retrieved the folder with the math paper for Hailey Granito; and found herself exhausted by lunchtime. Sitting at her usual table, she heard, "Hey, Lost and Found!"

For the first time the name kind of annoyed her. She hadn't been called Lost and Found all week, since she'd started searching with Jake, who didn't call her that anymore, she realized.

When she looked up to see who was shouting out to her, though, she saw that it was one of the kids at the table where Jake usually sat. His entire table of friends looked over at her, smiling, inviting.

Her head swiveled about for Jake and she saw him standing in the pizza line. He waved his hands around, some change falling out of them as he did, motioning for her to go sit with his friends.

For a brief instant, Tillie wondered if this was all a prank. Still, she got up, straightened her back as best she could, and made her way a few yards over to sit with a dozen laughing faces, some of which she had never seen up-close and in-person before. For a moment she wondered if any of them had been the ones who had laughed at Jake's impression of her in sixth grade . . . But she tried to shove that question out of her mind.

"You're always over there," said the girl on the end of the table who had called her over. Tillie knew her from her sixth-grade math and science classes: Abby Whatley. Tillie, red-faced, slid in next to her with her lunch tray.

"Yeah." Tillie laughed nervously.

"It's better over here," Abby Whatley continued, as if nothing out of the ordinary was going on, as if people just moved tables all the time.

Tillie hadn't sat with friends at lunchtime since Sydney and Zahreen.

"We're, like, three feet from the smoothies stand, and if the line ever shortens we rush it and get first dibs."

"Cool," was all Tillie could think of to say.

Abby Whatley's arm lifted and swung behind her. Startled, Tillie jumped in her seat a little, but it was just Jake standing behind them, high-fiving Abby in greeting. He looked wide-awake, energized, but his eyes were bloodshot, and Tillie spotted a small gray hair in one of his eyebrows.

"I see you've met Abby," Jake said. "Abby's always asking me about your pictures and stuff."

"What?"

"Oooh, yeah, let me see some!" Abby said, reaching for the camera. "The lost objects inside the prison walls of Hansberry Middle School!"

Abby's tongue stuck out of her mouth a little when she smiled.

Tillie flinched, but let Abby hold the camera. She kept it safe around her neck, though, and Abby's fingers bumped against the buttons on Tillie's brown cardigan as they examined the lens.

"Oh, no, no, not the lens, okay?"

"Oops, sorry!" Abby said.

Four other people asked to see it, too.

"Aw, man, you never let *me* touch it, and I love that

116

vintage-y old thing!" Jake said. He took a bite of pizza and yelled down the table, "Luke, check this old camera out!"

"Okay, okay," Tillie said, taking the strap off, suddenly surrounded. "But . . . but don't take any pictures with it, okay? And," she added under her breath, "it's not 'vintage-y.' It's just a full-frame DSLR with a 17-50 zoom lens, not some point-and-shoot or something." No one was listening, except Abby, who nodded her head as if she knew what Tillie was talking about.

Jake introduced her to all of them. She knew their names, of course—Luke, Emma, Lily, Sean, Sarah, Ian—and their faces had long been documented in the files on her laptop as they'd moved in and out of one another's social groups over the last year and a half, but they all said hi as if they'd never heard of her and she'd never seen them.

The crowd passed around her camera, ooh-ing and ahh-ing over its manual lens and "old-fashioned" look. It only seemed old-fashioned to them because it wasn't a phone. And besides, it was just a camera she had found at a yard sale, Tillie wanted to say, but she didn't know if that was impressive or cheesy.

Jake scooted in between Abby and Tillie as the cluster of kids yelled over one another to be heard. He leaned in toward Tillie, grabbed her arm, and whispered, "What class do you have next? I'll walk you there so we can talk."

As she turned to him she saw that not only were his eyes bloodshot, but they were puffy, too, as if he'd been crying.

Tillie tried not to stare as she told him it was art class with Ms. Martinez.

"The love of my life," Jake said with a mock lovelorn sigh, suddenly the opposite of the frantic person who had just whispered to her, turning back to his pizza crust, and, it seemed, his audience.

"The love of your life? Ew. You're obsessed," Abby said to Jake in a quick aside before returning to her own conversation.

Tillie surprised herself by joining in. "She *is* the greatest."

"Seriously," Jake said. "After parent-teacher conferences my dad said she should be an actress or something, not a teacher."

"Oh, because only ugly old witches should be teachers, with actual warts and stuff," Abby said, smacking Jake's arm.

"Yeah, and just because someone's really pretty it

doesn't mean they have to move to Hollywood or something," Tillie couldn't help but add.

"Wait a minute, whose side are you on here?" Jake protested.

"She's on the side of *reason*," Abby went on. "So old women should be teachers and pretty ones should be actresses or models or something? They have to fit nicely into little boxes based on their *appearance*? You're sexist."

"Totally," Tillie agreed.

"Okay, okay, stop ganging up on me!" Jake laughed and began to get up.

But his laugh wasn't like the night before. It sounded strained. Hollow.

As he picked up his tray he said quietly to Tillie, "Okay, come on, let's head out now and the hallways will be clear and we can talk."

Then he waved bye to his friends and tugged on Tillie's shirt a little, as if to pull her up.

She pushed his hand away.

He was always putting on a show, she realized. He obviously hadn't told his friends anything about his dad. Maybe he'd come to her because he was fake with the people who knew him. Watching him smile at his friends and then look to her with secret desperation, she wondered if there were times he'd just been pretending with *her* the past few days. This must be what he was doing at home, too, with his mom. It was a convincing performance. Tillie didn't like it.

This was one of the many reasons why being alone was easier—you didn't have to see all that was wrong with people. The antisocial life had its pluses.

Tillie took her camera back as several kids begged, "Pleeease let me take some pictures with it tomorrow!" Tillie nodded, but knew she wouldn't. *No one* took pictures with her camera but her. That would be like . . . someone else speaking with *her* voice. But she'd let them look at it again, if they wanted. She got up, leaving her tray, pulling her bad leg up at a weird angle. Without being aware of it, she must have grimaced, because Abby said, "Hey, are you okay?"

"Oh, I'm fine, totally," Tillie assured her as Jake, tapping his feet and fidgeting wildly behind her, motioned with his head for her to follow, and they made their way out of the cafeteria.

Jake led Tillie to the hallway corner. They dropped their backpacks at their feet and leaned against a locker. A few yards away from them, two eighth graders held hands and whispered. Toward the end of the hall, Cara

Dale put on some makeup in her locker mirror and flashed a hallway pass at an ornery hall monitor. Other than that, the hallway was empty.

Jake laughed again, but at nothing. The same empty laugh from earlier.

Tillie forced herself to scan his eyes and she saw they were wet.

"I was up all night," Jake said, his breath rapid and panicked. "I just . . . It's been a week now. And I still don't know where he is, ya know? And last night, I mean, it was crazy, but it didn't actually lead to anything. And it was stupid. I know. It was stupid. A waste of time." Jake smacked his own head.

"Hey," she said, putting a hand on his shoulder to quiet him, and then swiftly bringing it back down to her side. "I have an idea," she said as calmly as possible. "Let's look through the photos we have, okay?"

"Yeah, yeah, okay, okay." Jake nodded hard and fast.

"Can we sit?"

"Yeah."

They slid down the lockers and clicked through her photos.

School. Squirrels. Jim. Cubicle Man. Car. School.

Beside her, Jake's skinny legs wobbled side to side. He

bit his nails. It caught Tillie off guard how worried she felt about this behavior. About him. She wanted to make it all better. She wanted her pictures to fix everything.

"Wait," Jake said. "Go back to the car."

"It's too blurry. If you zoom in you can see most of the license plate number, but not the last digit."

"I know, I know, you said, but look." Jake grabbed the camera.

"Careful," Tillie warned as Jake furiously scanned the photos of the blue Chevy.

And then Tillie saw his whole body unwind. His limbs went still. He exhaled audibly. "Got something."

Tillie took the camera back and they looked together. All she saw was a blurry shot of the side of the car. "What?" Tillie asked, frustrated, seeing nothing.

"Zoom in on the window."

She did so. The inside of the car wasn't visible. The shot only revealed a reflection of light and a little white sticker in the bottom corner. A sticker . . . with bar codes. "The bar codes?" Tillie turned to him.

Jake smiled. A real smile this time, though his eyes still looked slightly crazed, like in a cartoon when spirals replace pupils. "It's a *rental*," he said. "The bar code sticker means it's a rental."

Tillie stared at the sticker. She hadn't known that

about cars (she didn't know anything about cars, and didn't particularly care to). But if Jake was right, then they had a path forward.

"Time to research Templeton rentals," Jake said as the bell rang, the cafeteria doors burst open, and a sea of kids swarmed the hallway. "How much you want to *bet* this leads us to Cubicle Man? I bet you anything."

They stood up.

"We have a lead," he murmured, more to himself than to Tillie. "We have a lead." Jake turned and bounded off to his next class.

Tillie moved slowly and steadily in the tidal wave of students. She turned toward the stairwell and clutched the stairway's banister as she headed toward art class. Out of pride, she'd long refused to take the school elevator. Some people really needed it. She didn't. One foot up. The other foot up to match. Repeat. Take a photo on each step. Repeat. Forget Jake's eyes. Repeat. Forget his bitten-down nails. Repeat.

When Tillie handed Ms. Martinez her collage, Ms. Martinez smiled, and said, "Look at that. Just lovely."

The mistakes *had* made it better.

As class started and a lecture on Matisse began, Tillie took out the small camera she'd brought in her pocket and, hiding the camera behind a propped-up textbook, she clicked through pictures from the past two weeks that might help in the search for Ms. Martinez's glasses. It was a search that might not be as exciting as a conspiracy or a night out in the darkness, Tillie thought, but it was one that wouldn't make her feel so many baffling, elating, exhausting things.

It was a lost thing no one would cry about if it couldn't be found.

11

Loner

TILLIE AND JAKE TEXTED ALL WEEKEND ABOUT the rental car.

i called a bunch of rental places, he texted her on Saturday. **asked if they rented out a blue chevy malibu recently. no help**

Understandable, Tillie responded. **They can't give out that info just like that . . .**

even tried my old man hausmann voice where i sound intimidating. no luck.

He sent her screenshots of spy and action movies. **they say you do your best learning outside of school,** he wrote, followed by a smiley face. **no seriously im learning some crazy stuff.**

Saturday night he tried to hack into his mom's email and see if she'd really been communicating with his dad.

i cant get in! he texted. **what kind of parent doesnt use their kids name or birthday for a password. whatever. now i search for those bank statements. maybe ill find something.** An hour later he added, **no luck.**

By Sunday he had grown unhinged.

over a week now. gone over a week. ten days. TEN DAYS!!!! he wrote at 10 a.m.

Only ten minutes later, he added: **my dad definitely saw cubicle man do something. or cubicle man is money hungry. but what does jim know? he must be in on it too.**

Around lunchtime, he wrote: **biking to my dads office. no one is there but I don't care. cant stay here. cant sit still**

Later in the afternoon, she received a series of non-sensical emojis—guy golfing, medical syringe, heart with a bow on it, Israeli flag, unicorn—followed by **freakin out freakin out freakin out**

On her end, she printed out the important photos in the case and put them all in chronological order. She wrote out a timeline of all the events as best she knew about them. She made a list of all the rental car places in town and noted which ones were close to Jake's dad's office so they could go to those first. But it *had* been ten days since he left home, and they weren't close to an answer, and a big part of her prayed that by the end of the weekend his dad would waltz through the door and say, "I'm home from my trip, son! Why would you have worried?"

Around dinnertime Jake started to call her multiple times, and she plugged in her phone near the kitchen and went to her bedroom to ignore it. Just for a little bit. She needed a break. She needed life to go back to normal for a few hours.

That night, as Tillie studied her pictures, she got a step closer to finding the missing glasses. Ms. Martinez had been wearing the lost pair, light brown with white polka dots, on March 8, a date recorded on the digital image. Tillie had a picture from that day of Ms. Martinez, her mouth frozen mid-sentence while she held up Deshaun's sculpture in her hand as an example to the class of how to portray movement, her glasses obscuring her nearly black eyes.

In a picture from the next day, taken when Tillie was waiting for the school bus to come, Ms. Martinez wore those glasses pushed up on her hair like a headband as she headed toward the faculty parking lot. But the next class, March 10, the day that they started to learn about cut-outs and collages, her brown glasses were replaced by her other pair. All Tillie had to do was ask Ms. Martinez where she went that day after the clay sculptures, and then go there, and ask around to see if a pair of glasses had been left by a pretty woman with dark hair. Maybe she'd get lucky.

The array of Ms. Martinez photos covered so much of Tillie's desk that some of them had slipped off onto the floor.

Tillie heard a light knock at her door.

"I'm busy!" she hollered.

The door opened. For once, it wasn't her mom.

"How's it going?" her dad asked her.

He looked at his feet just like she did, she saw.

"Pretty good," she answered.

"Great," her dad said.

Tillie attempted to cover the spread of the Ms. Martinez photos on her desk with her hands.

"Look, I know I said this the other day, but . . . But I'm really sorry I didn't take you to the doctor's."

"Huh?" Tillie said.

"The other day. I really am sorry," he answered. His big toe twitched up and down inside his sock.

"It's okay." She hadn't even been thinking about it.

"I will from now on."

"Okay," Tillie said. Her mom must have really gotten to him this time.

"No, Til, I just—"

Tillie waited for him to finish, but he didn't.

He paused, standing awkwardly by her door. "Oh, hey—lots of talk this week about the World Cup."

"Oh, yeah?"

"Yeah. Looks like it's going to be too hot, so they might have to move locations. Let's hope they bring it to Illinois, right?" Her dad chuckled.

"Well, I don't know much about it," she responded. She could hardly remember ever having been interested in soccer.

"Oh, of course. Sure."

"Well, not for any good reason," she added. It wasn't because of her leg that she didn't know, she wanted to say. She probably would've lost interest in soccer at some point, anyway, no matter what had happened. Come to think of it, her grandpa might've given her a camera at some point, accident or not. Maybe he just thought it suited her. And if he hadn't, she probably would've found photography in some other way. "Just not really my thing."

"Yes, of course. Okay, well, I'll take you to the doctor's next time, Til."

"Okay, Dad," Tillie said, wanting to believe him.

He started to leave but stopped, turned around again, and said, "Oh, and Vivian Maier was a photographer." He paused. "Her stuff is great."

"Really?" Tillie sat up a little straighter.

"Yeah." He smiled.

"What'd she like to take pictures of?" Tillie asked.

"People. People everywhere. Shopping, playing with their kids, working. And all kinds—rich, poor. She took . . . I mean, it must have been over a hundred thousand photographs. And this was on film, of course, not digital or anything."

"Wow," Tillie whispered.

"Yeah. But she never showed them to anyone while she was alive."

"Why?"

Her dad shrugged. "I don't know." After a beat he added, "She was a bit of an outsider. A loner, I think. Didn't want attention."

A loner, Tillie repeated in her head.

He nodded over and over like he did when there was nothing left to talk about. "Okay, Til, I'm heading to bed. Night." He closed the door, leaving her alone to exhale and let the pictures under her hands go free.

She had to print those pictures of her dad from that morning and search his face. Something was going on with him. Something new.

She had to sleep.

She had to learn more about Vivian Maier and her thousands of photographs.

She had to find out how to go from a bar code on a car window to an answer.

She had to . . .

Her mom knocked on the door and opened it. She held out Tillie's cell phone.

"I didn't pick it up," her mom said immediately, as if to stop any of Tillie's protestations before they began. "But that boy Jake is definitely trying to reach you. I wasn't snooping, I swear! I just saw his name when it lit up!"

Tillie let out a small laugh at her mom. "'*That boy* . . .'"

"What? I just—"

"I know, Mom. He's just a kid from school, okay?"

Her mom nodded. "Okay, sweetie." She paused. "You guys have sure been talking a lot. Maybe you should have him over sometime? We could meet him?"

"Sure, Mom," Tillie soothed her. "It's not like that, though."

"Whatever you say." Her mom's attempts at trying to

now be okay with the "boyfriend" she'd created for Tillie in her mind were so transparent it was funny. She blew Tillie a quick kiss and shut the door.

Tillie's phone vibrated in her hand. And then it vibrated again, and again.

"What's going on?" Tillie answered.

"Where have you been?"

"I was—"

But Jake cut her off.

"Forget all other leads. Forget everything else. It happened. He made contact." Jake was nearly hyperventilating. "He called and I picked up. And I know where he was calling from."

12

Don't Ask Questions

"HE CALLED ME FROM A NUMBER I DIDN'T KNOW," Jake told her. "At first I was like, 'Who is this?' and right away, there's breathing, and I know it's him. He said to me, 'I'm sorry, buddy, I have so much to tell you.' And then I asked him where he was and all he said was: 'I'll talk to you soon. Really soon. I promise.'"

"And then what?" Tillie asked.

"And then he hung up. He sounded really upset. Like he didn't have a lot of time."

"You said you know where he was?"

"Pins and Whistles. For sure."

Tillie's silence conveyed how meaningless this name was to her.

"The bowling alley, of course!" He'd been panting a little, but he started to settle down.

Tillie heard TV in the background, as usual. Her own parents were down the hall watching TV, too—their Sunday-night ritual.

"Okay, so how'd you know that's where he was? If it was an unknown number?"

"It was obvious," he said, and she could perfectly imagine his know-it-all look. "It had all the sounds of a bowling alley–karaoke place. And I only know of one. Don't you?"

"I never heard of any, actually. But okay." Tillie opened her laptop and looked up Pins and Whistles as they spoke.

"Oh, come on, you never went to birthday parties there or anything?"

"No." It wasn't that kids were trying to be mean when they'd stopped inviting her to things back in elementary school. It's just that after she hadn't been able to go for so long, they fell out of the habit of asking her to come.

"There were three things that gave it away," Jake began. "One, the sound of horrible singers 'performing' 'Piano Man.' Two, crashes and cracking sounds." Tillie heard Jake smack his hands together, illustrating. "I mean, I didn't hear anyone yell 'Strike!' but I may as well have. And then," he added, as if it were an afterthought, "I, uh, Googled the number. And it was the number for Pins and Whistles."

Tillie burst out laughing. "Google was a dead giveaway."

"We'll go there tomorrow. Right?" he asked her, not laughing along with her.

Tillie clicked the directions icon and saw that it would take nearly half an hour to reach Pins and Whistles on the edge of town. Still, she told him yes, and they made a plan.

But first . . . school.

The day went by excruciatingly slowly. At lunch Jake didn't even talk to her about any of his theories. They both just listened to his friends' discussion (about what they'd do to survive an alien invasion) and continually glanced up at the clock. If this bowling alley was a place his dad went, they might be incredibly close to finding him. There was nothing to discuss. They'd meet at the flagpole after school.

In art class that day Tillie told Ms. Martinez her conclusions about the glasses.

"The day we finished with the clay sculptures, huh?" Ms. Martinez said. "Quite specific. Okay, well, hmm . . ." She looked up and to the left with her lips pursed. She had on a mauvish-pink lipstick and her lips made a perfect oval.

"I think before I went home that day I may have stopped at the little deli on Main Street, two blocks from my house. I only guess that because I go there almost every day, for milk and bread and things like that. But other than that, I can't really remember. I was probably home."

"And you're sure you've looked everywhere in the classroom and your house?" Tillie asked.

"Yup," Ms. Martinez said. "Haven't seen any trace of them."

"They must have been lost at the deli, then!" Tillie exclaimed. "Or on the street, but let's hope not, because the deli is our best bet at finding them."

"You're my Sherlock!" Ms. Martinez smiled at her. The two nearly miniscule crinkles on the side of each eye tilted upward with her cheeks.

Tillie blushed.

"Okay," Ms. Martinez continued, "I'll go ask the deli manager if he's seen them. Thanks so much."

"No," Tillie jumped in. "No, I'll get them. It's, like, my job," she said, feeling silly immediately.

"It's okay," Ms. Martinez said as the bell rang and class was scheduled to begin. "I'll grab them later this week. The grandma glasses are fine for now. You just enjoy your afternoon, okay?" She winked, patted Tillie's arm, and went to the front of the classroom.

As soon as school ended, Jake and Tillie met at the flag-pole and headed to the bus stop.

"The bowling alley opens at two on weekdays," Jake said as he checked his phone to look at the time, "and it's almost 3:30." They had a long journey, and the bus was late. "Hopefully he wasn't in there already today, and we haven't missed him."

"Bowling alleys open at two?" Tillie asked. "Why so early? Don't people have work?"

Jake shrugged. "Lots of people out of work, I guess? Retired, maybe. My dad and his buddies have on-site visits sometimes, but I think once in a while they just say that and go do fun stuff instead."

He tapped his foot, staring off down the road in the direction the bus would come from.

A booming vroom could be heard in the distance, and Jake leaned his torso so far away from the bench to look down the street that he almost tilted over and fell. But it was just a moving van, and it passed them by.

"Did you tell your mom that your dad called?" Tillie asked.

"Nope. 'Course not. She thinks I buy her little business trip story about Dad. Happy-go-lucky Jake. Nothing wrong with him, ever," Jake said bitterly. "The bus is here!" He jumped up.

Tillie took a window seat and Jake squeezed in beside her.

"So, I was thinking," Tillie began carefully. "Maybe it's time to really confront your mom about all of this. Make her tell you the truth, if she knows it, or tell her the truth, if she doesn't."

"She'll just lie to me more, or to herself. " Jake shook his head.

Tillie's dad's spy story came to her mind. Maybe Jake's mom was entirely innocent. Maybe she was married to a person she actually knew nothing about.

"No. No, we're going to find him today," he said. "And we'll figure out how we can help him."

Jake said nothing more. Tillie could tell he was done with that conversation.

A wave of exhaustion consumed Tillie as she looked out the window and saw how far away they were getting from the center of town, from their school and both their neighborhoods. They were headed out toward the strip malls and side-of-the-road fast food chains and away from the coffee shops and residential areas dotted with tree-filled parks and moms strolling around the block with toddlers. Tillie hated to admit it, but it made her nervous to leave her college-town cocoon.

Jake started softly singing "Piano Man."

Embarrassed, Tillie glanced around the bus to see if any passengers had noticed, but no one had even looked up from their phones.

Jake started playing air-piano. Tillie let out a small snort.

At this, Jake's worried expression melted to his usual mischievous grin and he began to sing louder. He drummed on his knees, and then on Tillie's, and continued on this way until the bus arrived at Pins and Whistles.

"I'm sorry, but you can't sit here," the bartender said.

"It's not like I'm buying beer! For the love of God! I just want a Coke!"

They sat on high stools by a bar that looked over at a scattering of bowling lanes. Over to the right of the bar was a tiny wooden stage with a karaoke screen in front of it. A microphone lay on the wood, held together by duct tape. Jake had burst through the door, looking around wildly for his dad. But there were only three people there, bowling and scowling in Jake and Tillie's direction. Jake had headed over toward the bar and Tillie had followed.

"Kids aren't allowed at the bar. Those are the rules. They teach you about rules in school, right?" the bartender said.

"Okay, okay," Jake said. He leaned over to Tillie and grumbled, "Somebody woke up on the wrong side of the bar this morning, am I right?" Then he looked back to the bartender, who had clearly heard him and was not amused. "Alright, then, we'd like to buy a couple games. And some shoes. Where do we go to do that?"

"I—" *can't bowl!* Tillie almost said, before she felt Jake give her a light kick, and it was her bad leg, and she kicked him back with her good one.

"Do you have a guardian with you?" The bartender sighed.

"No," Jake said.

The bartender raised an eyebrow.

"But my dad's coming soon," Jake added quickly. "He'll be around any minute now. He hangs out here a lot, maybe you've seen him. Light blond hair? Well, maybe red, if you get it in the right light, my mom says. He's kind of got a small belly." Jake patted his stomach.

The bartender glanced toward the phone behind the bar. For a moment, Tillie wondered if he knew who they were, and if he remembered Jake's dad using that phone the night before. But it was more likely, she imagined, that he was about to call security, or ask for their parents' numbers, or just kick them out.

Jake was messing this up. And if this didn't lead to anything, he'd be devastated, and they'd have traveled all that way for nothing.

Tillie took a brave, deep breath. In her best impression of a confident, polite young woman, she said, "Sir, is it possible to start a game now, or should we wait until our guardian comes?"

The bartender softened as he turned to Tillie. "Sorry, sweetie. I can't let you guys play."

Tillie knew that adults could get fired easily, for all sorts of reasons, and that they couldn't just make their own rules in their workplaces. Her dad had been laid off once for breaking a work rule, back when Tillie was a baby and they lived in another town. He'd let a local newspaper run a story his boss had told him he couldn't, so they let him go. Jake couldn't expect this man to change the rules for him.

"Okay," she said. Jake sat up from his slumped posture, ready to argue more. "Thank you so much for your time." She spoke with the voice her mom used when she dealt with health insurance people on the phone right before she hung up and cursed.

"Well," the bartender said, looking around the sparse bowling alley as if he were being followed, "you can definitely use the karaoke machine without a guardian. But it's eight bucks for each half hour you use it, so . . ."

Tillie turned to Jake and they locked eyes. Did he have money? She didn't.

"Yeah, sure, okay, we'll pay right when my dad comes, thanks," Jake said. He grabbed Tillie's hand, almost pulled her off the stool, and hopped over to the stage.

"What's your master plan here?" Tillie whispered.

"Look, all we need is time," he whispered back, keeping one eye on the bartender. The bartender kept one eye right back on Jake. Tillie looked back and forth between them as they arrived at the karaoke stage.

"He came here yesterday, we know that," Jake went on. "But for what? Who knows? Maybe he's been coming here to meet with somebody who's helping him. Or maybe if someone's got control over him, they bring him here. Maybe he needed me to hear this place, to know where he was. I don't know. But we just need to wait out the night and see."

"You know I have to be home, right? I have to be home by like five. Five fifteen, at the very latest. They think I'm at Art Club on Mondays."

"We'll worry about that later," Jake said. "For now, we need to stall."

Jake went over to the karaoke machine and grabbed the big black book sitting on top of it. He sat cross-legged on the dusty carpet floor next to the stage and flipped through the song lists.

"What are you doing?" Tillie said, twisting her way down to him on the floor. She glanced up at the bartender and gave a little wave.

"I'm going to spend as much time as I can picking a song," he said. "To buy us time for my dad to show up. And then . . . and then we're going to see how many 'half hours' we can sing through without paying."

"How did you think we could stay here without money?" Besides bus fare, Tillie only had about three dollars and change.

Jake didn't answer her. He just moved through the pages of the song lists, muttering to himself. "No. Maybe. Too annoying. Too hard. No. Maybe."

Tillie knew Jake would have to sing pretty soon or the bartender might get annoyed with them and ask more questions. She watched the door, in case Jake's dad came through, and the bartender, in case he started to come over and see why they were just sitting around.

The group of three bowlers kept looking over at them and laughing. She wondered if they'd seen her limp. Or if they figured she and Jake were some kind of couple and thought it was cute. For half a second, she considered the idea that maybe they were kidnappers and were hiding Jake's dad somewhere.

"Jake, come on, you have to buy a song and sing something or we'll have to leave. We should probably just leave now anyway, this place is creepy!"

"Shhh. Just let the calm wash over you. Shhh."

"Oh, *now* look who's calm. All weekend you were—" Tillie took a breath. His faith that his dad would come there seemed to have given him a jolt of confidence. "Okay. Fine," she said. She'd do her job, fulfill her purpose. She lifted her camera up from her chest and snapped a picture of the sunken-eyed men watching them.

"We want a song!" one of the bowlers, scruffy and scrawny, yelled over, his words slurring a little.

"Yeah!" another one said, this one just as ragged-looking but rounder, with a too-tight shirt that exposed a slice of his large stomach. He chuckled and hit his friend's arm like he had said something hilarious. "Entertainment!"

"Yeah. Sing," the bartender added drolly from over at the bar.

It had only been about fifteen minutes since they had arrived, Tillie guessed, but other people had begun to pour in, and none of them were kids. This was not a place for kids at all, she noticed. She wondered what kind of birthday party Jake had been to there.

The cries for singing mounted. Even though it was really only a few stray voices taunting them, to Tillie it felt like a stadium.

"Okay, we have to do this." Jake picked up the small remote on top of the karaoke machine. Tillie heard a click as the machine turned on.

"You up for some Bob Dylan? The best of the best?" he asked her, clicking away.

"What?" Tillie rolled her eyes. "I don't really know any!" She tried not to sound as panicked as she felt.

"Okeydokey." Jake hopped up onto the stage. "That's a real shame, though. Alright, I got it." Jake pressed some more buttons before dropping the remote and picking up the microphone.

Tillie moved back, inching along the floor, her eyes shifting from one person to another to see who was looking. The three bowlers were still watching, along with an amused-looking man and woman in denim jackets sitting at the bar. The woman had a streak of hot pink in her bleached hair. Tillie moved toward a chair by the stage, nervous to watch Jake act foolishly. Committing a crime by stealing a karaoke song type of foolish. Tillie stared at the door looking for any sign of a dad of any sort as hip-hop beats began to rumble over the speakers.

"Jake Hausmann and Tillie Green, everybody," Jake said into the microphone. "Here we go!"

Tillie's head shot back to Jake. "What?" she yelled over the music. "I'm not coming up there!"

"It's a duet!" he yelled at her, covering the microphone with his hand. "Well, I think Jay Z's part counts as a duet . . ." he added, to himself. "And don't make me sing a duet alone!" he accidentally bellowed right into the microphone, as the lyrics to the spoken intro to the song began to float across the screen. As Beyoncé and Jay Z's "Crazy in Love" started, the screen played a video of cherry blossoms, a man reading a newspaper on an elevator, and a dog barking at the ocean. Karaoke was weird.

Tillie stood up and moved another couple of steps

away from Jake. She looked back at the bartender. He was staring.

"You're going to make me sing Beyoncé's part?" Jake asked her with his mouth away from the microphone as the beat of the song's intro continued. "Okay, fine," he said. "I'll be Queen Bey." Jake shrugged. "Gladly, in fact." And he lifted the microphone and began to sing.

Tillie couldn't believe what she was seeing. Or hearing. Jake had a voice that sounded positively church-worthy, Tillie thought with a snicker she didn't let out. Was he singing up an octave?

It was hilarious, Tillie had to admit. Watching Jake and the little side-step dance he was doing, listening to his soprano voice, she found it easy to ignore the hollers and hoots around them. Tillie absentmindedly inched close to the edge of the platform where Jake stood, and before she knew it he had pulled her up onto the stage next to him. Tillie faintly joined in the chorus along with him, her voice low and his high. She tried not to sing too loudly, to stay nice and quiet, but Jake moved the microphone closer to her mouth.

A musical interlude began and Jake stepped away from the microphone, do-si-doed around her and said into her ear, "Okay, it's your turn, Jay . . ." And though on a normal day almost nothing could possibly sound more terrifying than rapping Jay Z's verse from "Crazy in Love" into a microphone in front of real live humans, Tillie looked into Jake's laughing eyes and smiled. The fact that he managed to have laughing eyes even at a moment in which everything in his life was pretty much awful made her want to just forget all her hesitation, put her mouth toward the microphone, which smelled a little like horseradish and sweat, and do her best "Jay."

And she stumbled, but she made it through the whole verse.

When the melody returned, Jake jumped right back in. He attempted an Elvis thing with his hips and gave her a thumbs-up sign as the final chorus began. They sang "crazy in love" over and over again as the music built to a joyful burst.

A tiny crowd had formed in front of them, by the bar. The stragglers waiting for their drinks bobbed their heads to Beyoncé and Jay Z, Jake and Tillie.

As they finished the last line, a couple of people whistled.

The music began to fade. Tillie turned to look at Jake, but all she saw was space. The music stopped and the karaoke machine went static. Tillie spotted Jake making his way away from her and toward the bar.

"It's you!" Tillie heard Jake say, out of breath, his voice cracking, at the corner of the bar a few feet away.

Tillie tried to move carefully off the stage, but in her rush to get to Jake she tripped off the small corner of the stage platform. Involuntarily, she yelled out in pain. The woman with the pink streak in her hair rushed to help her. On her knees by the wooden planks of the stage, Tillie felt an ache in her ankle creep up the back of her leg toward her spine.

"Jake!" she called out. She still couldn't see who he was talking to. Jake and whoever-it-was were hidden by the small group of people who had been bobbing their heads. Was it his dad? Had they finally found him?

"What's going on here?" She heard the bartender yell, and she tried to crawl a bit toward where Jake stood, but it hurt.

"You know where he is and you're not telling! What did you do to him?" Tillie heard Jake shout.

As the woman rubbed Tillie's back and pulled her hand to help her up, Tillie saw what was happening.

Cubicle Man was at the bar.

"I know about you! I know all about you!" Jake screamed. "You did something to my dad! You know where he is!"

"I don't know what you're talking about!" Cubicle Man yelled back, trying to get away from Jake, who had started pushing him. "Get this kid away from me!" he hollered.

Tillie began to snap picture after picture, ignoring the questions of the woman behind her, asking her what she was doing and where her parents were.

"What was it, huh?" Jake shouted. "Did you think we had money? Well, we don't, so let my dad go!"

"This is ridiculous!" Cubicle Man seethed.

"Did he catch you doing something? Huh?" Jake followed the man as he tried to escape.

The bartender made his way toward Jake.

"You were the guy stealing office supplies, weren't you? Did you steal something else? Are you a thief? I know about you! I know all about you!"

Tillie recognized that Jake was out of control. She nearly hurled herself across the room to get to him, her adrenaline masking the warning of the pain sure to come.

"You need to stop!" Cubicle Man fumed.

The bartender reached Jake and pulled him up by the back of the shirt. "Get out of here," he said.

As Tillie neared Jake, Cubicle Man caught her eye.

She was still several feet away from Jake and couldn't avoid walking past Cubicle Man to get to him. She felt her whole body tighten as she moved forward.

"Jake! I'm coming!"

And then she felt someone grab her by the arm. She snapped her head around.

"Stop asking questions you don't really want to know the answer to," Cubicle Man said to her in a raspy whisper. "Trust me."

He *did* have a scar above his eye, stark white, cutting slightly into his eyebrow. Tillie jerked her arm away and made it to Jake. He was fighting with the bartender at the door.

"Don't come back, Destiny's Child, or I'm calling the cops," the bartender said as he shoved Jake out the door and motioned for Tillie to follow.

Jake tried to run back toward the entrance, but Tillie did what the bartender had done, and dragged Jake away by his shirt.

✳ ✳ ✳

"I can't believe that creep was there," Jake moaned. "I can't believe he was there, and I didn't get anything out of him."

He rubbed his temples over and over as if he wanted to reach inside his head and strangle his own mind.

Tillie had led Jake, ranting and raving, back to the bus stop, breathing so heavily that she could hear his inhales over the traffic.

The bus ride home was so long. Her mom would be worried. If the bus came soon, she could *maybe* make it home on time. Or at least be only a little late. Tillie texted her mom that she'd be home really soon, that Art Club had run over again, that everything was fine. And then she turned back to Jake.

"Tillie, that was him, wasn't it? *That was him!*"

She nodded. She had studied his face a million times in nights spent poring over her pictures. The man at Pins and Whistles had the same sloped, bald head, the same small glasses, the faint scar. And he'd been furious at the sight of Jake. When she'd taken this man's photo, and seen the finger against his lips, she'd told Jake she believed him that something was going on, and she had. But it was only now, after Cubicle Man grabbed her arm to silence her, too, that she was entirely certain that Jake was right. His dad wasn't in Canada. He wasn't on a trip. Jake's dad was *lost*. Taken?

"And he was at the same place my dad called from!

The day after he called!" Jake lamented. "Tillie, he did something to him. I know it."

"Yeah, he's definitely involved. You're right." Tillie pictured his dark eyes as he growled at her.

Stop asking questions . . .

"Yeah, and he got away," Jake whimpered. "He got away . . ."

The sun would set soon, and Tillie pulled her jacket more tightly around herself. Her leg and hip throbbed. She reached in her bag for some camphor, which her mom always packed, and slipped off her sock and sneaker, accidentally pulling out her heel lift with it. She pushed the shoe insert back in and began to rub away the muscular strain in her heel. The balm would make her colder, but it would take away some of the effects of the painful fall off that stupid karaoke stage. When she reached up under the leg of her jeans to put some on her calf, she glanced at Jake, self-conscious that he would witness all this, and saw that he was shaking.

Jake held his face in his hands. His shoulders trembled like earthquake aftershocks, one huge heave of breath followed by small rippling tremors. His backpack had started to fall off his shoulders and it pulled on his arms.

Tillie had never seen a boy cry before. Maybe when she was a little kid, or back when her dad visited her in the hospital, but that was different.

Jake said something unintelligible.

"What?" Tillie asked softly.

"I'm not going to find him," he said, with so much articulation that it looked like it wore him out, and he couldn't talk more.

Tillie tried not to stare.

She moved her hands to his backpack straps and slipped them off each arm. He let her. His face was wet, his tears reflecting the lights of the cars that went by.

Tillie took his backpack and set it down near her sore foot.

"Are you okay?" she asked.

He nodded. His breath slowed.

Tillie thought for sure they would never talk again after this moment. That if a boy cried in front of you then that was it, that was the end. It was just too awkward to go on. The investigation would be over, and Cubicle Man and his lackey, Jim, would get away with everything. But she was immediately proven wrong. Jake began to speak.

"My dad is my best friend," he said, glazy-eyed, sniffling

and wiping his nose with his coat sleeve. "Do you know what I mean?" he asked, but he didn't wait for an answer.

And no, she didn't know.

He let out a pathetic little laugh. "I found a card the other day that I wrote him. I've been looking in Mom and Dad's room. For, you know, clues. Or anything I can find. And I found a card. It was in his nightstand drawer. It was a card from me, for his birthday. I was nine. It says 'Happy birthday, Dad! I don't know what I'd do without you.' And I didn't. I mean, it's because of my dad that I learned to, like . . . *like* myself, I guess. Because *he* liked me so much. And the thing is . . ." He paused, biting his lip and pushing his hands together to fight more tears. "I'm not nine anymore, and I still don't know what I'd do without him. But now I *am* without him. And I'm . . . nothing." Jake paused again. "I'm nothing without him." He shook his head and wiped under his eyes. Then he said, low and to himself, "I just want my dad back. I just want back that one person who tells me everything's going to be okay, and who means it."

Tillie knew the words wouldn't mean much coming from her, so she just thought them. *Everything's going to be okay, Jake.* And then she had to stop thinking about it, or she knew she might cry, too.

After what felt like an eternity, the bus came, and they headed home.

That night her dad heated up a pork chop for her for dinner.

She wanted to hug him, but instead she asked him to pass the salt.

13

That Face

JAKE WASN'T AT SCHOOL THE NEXT MORNING, OR the day after that.

The first day, he texted Tillie that he had stayed home to investigate, though Tillie imagined he mostly needed to recover from their awful night. The second day, he didn't text at all. And Tillie started to worry.

Abby told Tillie he'd texted her that morning to tell her he was still sick. After stopping Tillie on her way to Ms. Martinez's room and insisting that she eat lunch with "their group" instead, Abby told Tillie all kinds of things. She told her she'd had a crush on the eighth grader Malik Granger for two years, that it annoyed her that he was probably in love with Diana Farr just like everyone else, that she was looking to start a band and if

Tillie played any instruments she should join, and all kinds of theories about the characters on a TV show Tillie had never watched but Abby insisted "she had to." Abby didn't even walk ahead of Tillie, she just strolled slowly alongside her, even as her words moved a million miles a minute.

"Jake was right," Abby said as they walked into the cafeteria. "You're a really good listener."

It felt weird to sit at Jake's table without him, but Abby acted like Tillie was entirely welcome. She talked to Tillie, but also to everyone else.

"Hey, if my band works out do you think you could take publicity shots for us or something?" Abby asked her at one point, initiating a whole discussion at the table of all the things people needed pictures for. Sean wanted a headshot for a community theater production he planned on auditioning for, and Emma wanted to make sure someone took a good photo of the girls' basketball team for yearbook because the year before they'd all hated it.

Tillie, shocking herself, said yes to all of it. She relaxed into her spot at the table without Jake by her side.

Then, at one point, Abby put her hand to her mouth and said, "Oh, I totally forgot. I should be collecting

Jake's homework for the classes I have with him. He asked me to . . . Oops."

Tillie felt guilty that for a moment, while chatting with Abby, she'd forgotten Jake. She'd forgotten his heaving breaths, and how he'd clenched his hands so tightly his knuckles turned white.

"Yeah, I hope he's okay," Tillie said, meaning something else entirely.

Tillie wished Jake would just talk to his mom. Was his mom still maintaining that his dad was on a business trip? How long did she expect that obvious lie to work? Tillie could imagine, though, that Jake had convinced her of his blissful ignorance. He was probably all smiles and jokes.

Tillie texted him. **Hey, when can we discuss Monday night's evidence?**

She tried not to let it bother her that he'd texted Abby and not her.

By her next class, he hadn't texted back. She saw Abby in the halls. Well, really, she put herself near Abby's locker to make sure she'd run into her.

"Hey, you heard from Jake?" Tillie asked her.

"Not since this morning. He's probably busy playing some role-playing game on the computer or something equally nerdy." Abby rolled her eyes and smiled.

"Huh," Tillie said.

"Why?"

Tillie didn't know what to say.

After that night, there was no way that Cubicle Man didn't know Jake was onto him—about whatever it was Cubicle Man had done. And it was obvious that Cubicle Man didn't just know something about where Jake's dad was, but he had something to do with his disappearance. Maybe he'd hurt him for some reason. Maybe he was threatening Jake's mom. And if he knew Jake knew . . . then was Jake in any kind of danger? Was Cubicle Man *that* menacing? Was the action movie Jake had imagined actually coming true?

And why was his mom still lying? Tillie wondered. Was she really just protecting Jake? That part made no sense to her.

Tillie pictured Jake's red, tearstained face two nights before. This couldn't go on. She couldn't bear for him to feel like that any longer.

"Hey, Abby, do you know Jake's address by any chance?"

"Yeah, totally. Hand me your phone, I'll put it in. Why?"

"Thanks," Tillie mumbled. "Just . . . stopping by." Tillie handed Abby the phone. She had to convince Jake to tell his mom what he knew. They needed help with all of this before Cubicle Man had the chance to do any more damage.

"Hey, if you're going over there, I'll come along!" Abby announced. "It'll be fun! Oooh, let's get him some soup first or something. A care package! His mom won't care, she hardly pays attention to what he does, anyway. And his dad will just, like, join in the fun."

It hit Tillie in a new way that Jake hadn't told any of his friends about his dad. Of course, she'd known that all along. That was why he was always whispering with her while laughing loudly about other stuff with them. But she suddenly understood that, for some reason, Jake really trusted her.

Tillie became aware she was just standing there, staring at Abby, thinking, and she scolded herself inside for being so weird.

"Um . . ." Tillie couldn't let her join. Abby couldn't get involved in all this, especially considering how frightening it seemed to be getting. "Sorry, I—"

"Oh. No, no, it's totally okay. No worries, I get it." Abby pasted on a smile.

"Sorry," Tillie repeated.

"Hey . . ." Abby's smile faded as she lowered her voice.

"Something's obviously going on with Jake. And I've seen you guys whispering. You clearly know about it. Look, I get it if you can't say anything. But . . ." She paused as if waiting for Tillie to jump in, but Tillie didn't. She couldn't. "Just let me know if I can help. Or if *you* need someone to talk to." Abby lingered for a second, and then waved and headed off. "Okay, have a good one, Tillie!"

Abby was so nice, Tillie thought, and she herself was so, *so* awkward.

Cursing herself, she texted her mom on her way to her last class.

Might be running late tonight. I have a group project for Art Club and we're working in the library after school today.

Tillie winced. Art Club stuff every day all of a sudden? Not persuasive. Jake was much better at this sort of thing.

After school, she took the bus to Jake's house.

She didn't want to ambush him, so as she got off the bus she texted again:

I have some thoughts. Might come by? See you soon . . .

He lived by a soccer field where she used to have Rec and Ed soccer games, she realized as she walked from the bus stop to his street. She wondered if Jake ever played. He didn't seem too sporty . . .

The sidewalks were fairly empty, with only a couple of kids returning to their homes after school or running outside to jump on their bikes. A few women walked by with their dogs, spotted Tillie and her legs, and quickly looked the other way. The typical reaction. Tillie kept her eyes on the sidewalk straight ahead.

As Tillie neared Jake's house, she halted.

Three houses down from where she'd frozen, she saw a bald man in a suit, wearing glasses, knocking fiercely on Jake's door.

It couldn't be . . .

He put his hands on his hips, looked up in the air, shook his head in great annoyance, and knocked again. It was Cubicle Man.

What if he saw her?

Tillie dipped into the front yard she was closest to and headed for one of the bushes. Praying that no one in the house noticed, Tillie used one hand to move a branch out of the way and the other to hold her camera, but her arm began to shake, so she gave up. She couldn't get a shot. But spying on her parents had been great practice, and Tillie found her own peephole through the bush branches.

The door opened.

Jake's mom came out onto the porch holding a large duffel bag with a Cubs logo on it. She set it down in front of Cubicle Man. The bag was stuffed to the brim and something started to fall out of it—a baseball cap, maybe, Tillie couldn't be sure—and Jake's mom leaned down quickly to push it back in.

Jake's mom appeared to have no fear at all. She edged herself closer to Cubicle Man. Her arms gesticulated wildly. The two of them stood nearly nose to nose. Cubicle Man hunched over for a moment, like a caught child getting into trouble, but then he sprang up, shouting. Jake's mom stepped back. Tillie could hear Cubicle Man yelling, but the only words she could make out were "Fine, fine," and then she thought she might have heard him say, "What's done is done."

And then Tillie, who trusted her eyes so profoundly, couldn't believe what she saw: Cubicle Man and Jake's mom hugged. It only lasted a brief moment, but it happened.

Afterward, Cubicle Man took the duffel bag and walked away with it. He disappeared around the corner. Jake's mom watched him go for a moment, and then went back inside the house.

Could Tillie follow him? Maybe . . . No, she couldn't walk that fast.

She had more questions than ever. What was in the bag? Was it money? Was this what the bank statements had been about after all, paying a large sum? But why would there be a baseball cap on top of money? And why would they have hugged if Jake's mom didn't want to give him her money, or whatever was in the bag? *Was Jake's mom involved in all this? Was she on Cubicle Man's side?*

Tillie's body seemed to know what to do before she did. She found herself walking toward the house.

She walked up the steps of Jake's house to his door and knocked.

Within seconds Jake's mom opened the door.

His mom had a stern face. She had olive skin, but it clearly hadn't seen much sun lately. Her collarbone jutted out like a mannequin's. There was no pink to her cheeks. Her hair, wisps of faded brown dye, clung to her forehead, and navy-blue circles nestled under her eyes. She looked as if all the tears had been twisted out of her like a dried-out dishrag. This was not the woman Tillie had imagined. Jake had said she seemed fine.

"Can I help you?" his mom said without a trace of the warmth that Jake always had.

"Oh, um," Tillie said. "Yes?" she asked as a question. "I'm Jake's friend?" A question again. The word "friend" came out of her mouth as if she were looking it up in a foreign-language dictionary and trying to see if the native speaker understood it.

"He's not here."

Tillie paused. "He's—" She didn't want to say she had been told he was sick because maybe he'd lied to his mom as well. Maybe he was doing something else. She couldn't let his mom know. "Oh, I didn't bump into him at school today. And . . . we have a project together. I thought we could work on it now?"

"He's at Art Club," his mom said. "He was sick, but started to feel better around last period."

"Oh, yeah, okay. Art Club. Yeah, he's a great artist." Tillie hid a snicker.

"Okay," his mom said as she began to close the door. "I can tell him you stopped by."

But she hadn't even asked for Tillie's name.

As Tillie left Jake's doorstep, she texted him.

Jake, where are you???

She didn't want to give him any of this information in a text. She had to talk to him. She had to explain what she'd seen. But she didn't even know what she *had* seen.

She couldn't go home. What would she do, go home

and wait and see if Cubicle Man happened to hurt Jake? Wait and see if his mom was behind all of this somehow? None of these questions could wait another day. But she had nowhere to go.

Tillie walked back to the bus, still unsure of her next move. Her leg and hip were starting to tingle, perhaps from the overuse but maybe from the stress.

She'd go downtown. Since there was no Art Club, there was no way he was at school. Maybe he'd met up with his friends on Main Street. She cursed herself for not getting Abby's number. After she checked Main Street, she'd go to his dad's office, see if he'd gone there. But what if Cubicle Man was there? What if he'd returned to work, pretending to have just been out on one of those "on-site visits" Jake told her about? She couldn't be seen there. Neither could Jake! She had to find him.

When she stepped off the bus onto Main Street, she peered into the café where she knew kids hung out after school. Inside, she saw several groups of her classmates, including Diana Farr. Instinctively, Tillie took a picture. Cara Dale, a new recruit into Diana Farr's clique, saw her and giggled. Tillie wasn't positive the giggling was about her, but she thought it probably was. Pushing it out of her head, she went to the front of the store to get a hot chocolate.

Now all she could do was sit there and wait for a while to see if maybe Jake showed up. Tillie pulled out her camera and absentmindedly clicked through some of her favorite shots. The images drowned out the chatter in the café. Tillie came upon the portrait of Ms. Martinez. It wasn't a great picture, but she'd kept it on her camera because it brought her back to that day in the car, to Ms. Martinez telling her that her pictures were beautiful.

Ms. Martinez lived only a few blocks away, actually, Tillie remembered, clicking back to the previous picture of Ms. Martinez's house. Clareview Street.

What if, instead of getting Jake to tell his mom, she just told Ms. Martinez everything? She would know what to do. She wouldn't let anything happen to them. Jake might be mad at Tillie for it at first, but he would forgive her. He'd forgive her when he learned about the duffel bag and understood how real things were getting, and how it wasn't just a theory anymore. Now there was a bag full of . . . *something*, and a scary guy, and too many secrets, and she had to do something right then and there.

Tillie left her still-full hot chocolate, and headed out of the café toward Ms. Martinez's street.

Tillie texted her mom: **Running super late! Feeling fine, took some meds, pain not bad.**

Her mom texted back: **Hurry home, honey.**

A couple of blocks before Clareview, Tillie saw Ms. Martinez's Main Street deli and made a detour to go in. If she could grab Ms. Martinez's glasses, she figured, it could only help. It would give Tillie an opening, and since Ms. Martinez would be happy to get them, maybe she'd be more likely to listen to Tillie as she told her this outrageous-sounding story of the missing dad.

The deli was fairly empty. It had a handful of small tables to sit at, but no one was there. Black marks from customers' shoes covered the tile floor, and in the corner Tillie noticed some spilled ketchup. The place smelled like pickles. The man behind the register didn't seem to notice her come in, or perhaps he just didn't care. He leaned against the counter on his elbows, sighing every now and then, flipping the pages of a magazine. The boy behind the sandwich counter sat on a chair against the wall, asleep. A fly buzzed under his nose and Tillie took a picture of him sniffing in his sleep as it circled him.

Tillie hobbled toward the man behind the register. Her leg was starting to really bother her. Her lower back, too.

"Help you?" he said, looking up from his magazine.

"I—" Tillie started to answer.

"Oh, hey, what happened to your leg?" he asked.

People asked this a lot, as if it were their business. Usually she answered, "Oh, nothing, just recovering from a broken foot," which was a lie that made people comfortable. She'd long fantasized about making up something exciting, like "I was attacked by a mountain lion," or "I'm part pirate—there's an old-fashioned peg leg under my pants."

"Broken foot," she answered.

"Ah, I'm sorry. I broke my foot once." He leaned toward her and proceeded to tell her all the details of his baseball injury.

"So, um," she interrupted him, "I'm sorry, but I'm looking for some glasses?" She felt herself blush like she usually did when she asked someone for something.

"Everyone's losing their glasses, huh?" he asked, and shook his head.

"Huh?" Tillie said. "They're brown? With polka dots."

As she said "dots," the man spoke over her. "Ah, same pair. Some guy got those already."

A part of Tillie felt a little pleasure that she had been right—the glasses *had* been at the deli, just as she'd deduced from her photos. But this information also confused her. Some *guy*?

"Yeah," the man continued, "wrapped 'em up in some of our napkins here and stuffed 'em in a bag. Didn't say 'thank you' to me when I handed them over, but whatever. He was a Cubs fan, so I guess that's to be expected." The guy laughed. "Go Sox, right, kid?"

"Wait," Tillie said. "How'd you know he was a Cubs fan?"

"Cubs bag. Smug face."

Tillie took a breath. Just because it was a Cubs bag didn't mean it was the same guy. Maybe Ms. Martinez just had a boyfriend with a Cubs bag.

But maybe, for some reason, Cubicle Man was a step ahead of her. Maybe he was sending her a message. Maybe he knew she'd seen him at the house and wanted to remind her not to "ask questions." Maybe he was watching her right then.

Her stomach tightened and her bad leg began to quake. "Um," Tillie squeaked. "Did this guy have glasses, by any chance? Beady little eyes? Wearing a suit?"

"Ha! Descriptive." He smiled at her. "Glasses, yeah. Didn't exactly gaze into his eyes."

Tillie swallowed. "Was he bald?"

"Couldn't tell. He was wearing a baseball cap. Wait, are you the real live Nancy Drew? Right here in this deli?"

The man cackled. "What's the mystery? The Case of the Missing Glasses? The Secret of the Empty Suit?"

Tillie felt the world swirling around her. "Thank you!"

She hurried out.

"Good luck, Nancy!" the man yelled, still belly-laughing, and she could hear his howls even as the door dinged and closed behind her.

Jake, Tillie texted, **Cubicle Man is up to something. Sure of it. Seriously, where are you???**

Should she be even more worried about him than she already was? Cubicle Man might know *all about them*. He might have been following them around this whole time. He must have been the one driving the blue Chevy—he'd followed Jake to school and tailed them to the bus stop; who was to say he hadn't tracked them *everywhere*? Maybe he knew Ms. Martinez was their favorite teacher, that Tillie was the Lost and Found, that she was supposed to find the glasses. Was he watching her right then? Would he hurt Ms. Martinez to send some kind of awful message to stay away?

Tillie tried to move quickly, her backpack and camera clunking against her back and chest, her hair flying around her face in a whirlwind with each step. It wasn't far, she could make it, she told herself. Tillie tried to ignore that her leg hurt more than usual. It remained tender from the karaoke fall two nights before, and from the tension her body felt as it pushed itself faster than normal.

She passed a few kids from her school at one point and kept her head down. If they had any requests for the Lost and Found she just didn't have the time to spare.

When Tillie arrived at the corner of Main Street and Ms. Martinez's block, where she could see the little house, a man bounded out from behind her, nearly knocking into her with his shoulder, and walked right on ahead of her.

"'Scuse me," the voice said cheerily, but the kindness in his tone didn't stop Tillie from feeling like she'd been punched in the gut.

Tillie stopped in her tracks for a moment. She could see from the back side of him that he wore a baseball cap. Over his shoulder he carried an overstuffed duffel bag with the Cubs logo on it.

It was him. She hadn't seen his face, but it *had* to be him.

Had he recognized her? Maybe he hadn't really looked at her. He'd already moved several yards ahead.

Tillie kept going, but slowed down. If he turned around, if it was really him, she couldn't let him see her. She went into her incognito mode—a method she'd perfected by the end of elementary school—head down, hands on her backpack straps, turtle-like movements. She stayed far enough behind him that she had plausible deniability if he accused her of following him, but if he turned around and recognized her it was all over, anyway. She hid her face with her hair.

Tillie was a ways behind him when she saw him slow down right in front of what she recognized as Ms. Martinez's house.

She could hardly breathe. The man stopped at Ms. Martinez's mailbox and began to open it.

Was Ms. Martinez in danger? Tillie wondered if she should give her a warning of some kind. Should she yell out? But then he might come for her. Maybe that's exactly what he wanted. With his back still toward Tillie, he opened the mailbox and took out some envelopes. Wasn't it a federal crime to open someone else's mail? Her mom had told her that once, when she'd opened up something meant for her dad. *He'd better not open Ms. Martinez's mail,* Tillie thought. She'd report him.

. . . And then what?

Tillie felt helpless. Entirely and utterly helpless. There was only one thing she could do. Tillie lifted up her camera and began to document all of it. Keeping her distance, she took two shots and readied herself to drop her camera at a moment's notice if he saw her. But he was still looking down at the mail. He flipped through it as if he had all the time in the world, which helped Tillie, because she was stuck either standing there, or eventually moving forward and having to confront him, or hiding behind a tree or a car.

As he began to turn and head toward the house, Tillie chose the car. She took three steps to hide behind the vehicle parked in front of Ms. Martinez's neighbor's house, and she crouched down, perching her camera's lens above the hood. For the second time that day, she hid like a spy.

Ducking down low, Tillie came face-to-face with the car window. And when she saw a bar-coded sticker, she felt all the breath go out of her. Tillie was hiding behind *a rented blue Chevy*, parked mere yards from Ms. Martinez's home. She held on tight to her camera and told herself to focus.

Tillie took some shots of the man's back as he walked up the little concrete path that led to the house's front door. The man pulled some keys from his pocket and began to put them in the lock. He fumbled a bit.

Why did he have her keys?

Tillie had to do something. She had to scream.

Then the door opened. Ms. Martinez, out of her work clothes and in sweatpants and a hoodie, stood there smiling. She said something to the man and they both laughed. The man leaned down, opened the duffel bag, and pulled something out: the glasses, wrapped in deli napkins. Ms. Martinez laughed in delight. She gazed at him adoringly as he slid the glasses onto her face.

Tillie felt so stupid. This was all a coincidence. It wasn't Cubicle Man. No one was after Tillie or Ms. Martinez. It was just a boyfriend. The obvious answer. He happened to have a Cubs bag and a baseball cap because this was Templeton, Illinois, and everyone loved the Cubs and that was that. Ms. Martinez simply had a doting boyfriend running errands for her, because *of course* she did.

Ms. Martinez took a step out of the doorway and fell into the man's arms. He held her, and they kissed. A long, lingering kiss. And then she put her head on his shoulder, and the man, taller than her, rested his head on top of hers, with his face tilted so that Tillie made out his smiling profile.

And she knew that face.

176

It was the face of the happy man, the hilarious man, the man who put his loving arms around his wife and son in front of a lovely white house made for a perfect family.

It was Jake's dad.

14

This New You

"WHERE HAVE YOU BEEN?" TILLIE'S MOM SCOLDED when she arrived home. "You look exhausted. What happened?"

Tillie went toward her bedroom, silent. She dragged her limp foot and felt it fill up with pain with each graze upon the floor.

Her mom grabbed her shoulders and turned her around. They were in the doorway to the hall that separated their bedrooms from the kitchen and living room, and Tillie thought of Ms. Martinez standing in the doorway. She felt sick.

"Mom, let me go."

Her mom did.

"Excuse me, Miss Tillie, you are going to tell me where you were."

Her mom's arms formed perfect triangles on each side of her torso. She looked so angry it almost made Tillie laugh.

"What's that smirk about?" her mom said, close to yelling.

Tillie moved past her mom and made it to her room, her mom right behind her, speaking into the back of her head the whole way.

"Tillie, there is no Art Club, is there? Okay, fine, I'll tell you the truth, even though you never tell it to me. I *know* there's no Art Club. I know there isn't. I was trying to let you lie. To let you be . . . normal. Not that I mean you're not normal. I mean that I was letting you get away with this one. With your boyfriend. Which, yes, I know I need to learn is okay, because, of course, there will be more of them. Of course there will. But I check on these things, Tillie; I call. I call the school and find out when to pick you up and—guess what?—there's no Art Club. But I didn't say anything last night, did I? Did I? But this is several times in a row and I don't accept this anymore."

Tillie threw her backpack on the floor. She removed her camera from where it hung around her neck and gently placed it on her shelf. She pulled the small camera out of her coat pocket and put it next to the other one. She threw her coat on the floor. And she collapsed on the bed.

Her mother took in a sharp breath.

"Are you okay? Okay, I'll stop being angry. Just tell me you're okay."

Her mom leaned down to touch her leg, as if by placing her hand on it she could somehow tell how much pain Tillie was in. But Tillie kicked her mom away with her good leg, almost hitting her in the shoulder.

Her mom stood up, moved away from the bed, and choked out, "I hate this, Tillie. Whatever this is, these last couple weeks. This new you who is always gone. I'm so afraid for you. You struggle with movement, we know that. And all of a sudden you're out there somewhere, probably running all around, and I see you're in more pain than usual." Tillie's mom's voice broke for a moment. She dabbed under her eyes with the end of her sleeve. "And there's a cause and effect, honey. And you know, I leave work at four so I can come home for you. Do you realize that? And then you're not here. Do you know how much that hurts me, Tillie? Let alone worries me?"

Tillie rolled onto her side so that all she could see was the wall. "Go away, Mom," she said. "Please."

"Honey—"

"*Go away!*" Tillie yelled.

Her mom must have obliged, because Tillie felt herself fall asleep. She hadn't taken a nap since she was a little kid, but it felt warm and sweet.

When she woke up, her mom and dad were sitting in the kitchen with half-eaten suppers before them. Tillie wandered in looking for some kind of wake-up snack. She didn't even know what time it was.

As she made her way to the fridge, they were both staring at her.

"Tillie," her mom said. "We would like to talk to you."

Tillie grabbed a ginger ale and some cheese and sat down across from them at the kitchen table.

"Where were you, sweetie? Is something wrong?"

Tillie shook her head. "I was out taking pictures," she answered truthfully.

Her mom nodded, watching Tillie cut a huge slice of cheese and chomp it down. She was starving.

"Look, you know you can't be running around," Tillie's dad said. "If you get hurt more, we just won't be able to . . ." He trailed off. "To . . . I won't be able . . ." And then he didn't say anything. He was mute, as usual. He couldn't finish, though Tillie was dying for him to do just that.

"Yes?" she made herself say, still not looking at either of them. "Won't be able to . . . ?"

Her dad shook his head.

"I'm fine." She took a couple more bites, stuffing her mouth, and then got up from the table. Her parents were still silent, and she hated that she had to stagger back in front of them, in front of her dad, especially. She hated that she couldn't just walk straight.

When she got back to her room she saw she finally had a text from Jake. A long one.

hey. sorry. u ok? somehow last night mom found out about the bowling alley?? very very weird. do i have a microchip implanted in me or something? kidding kidding. obvs. phone got 'confiscated.' snuck into her room to write to abby and ian this am while she worked from home. now shes watching tv so i can check it. what's up w cubicle man? have new theory? i call u 2morrow. now i delete this and live a life of solitude ps even tho mom thought i was sick she still let me go to art club cuz i said i was super invested in the subject matter. hilarious. but guess where i was? that's right—a

rental place. got stuff to tell you tomorrow. k c ya soon matilda green

She put the memory card from her camera into her laptop, imported the photos, and pressed print.

The pictures of Ms. Martinez and Jake's dad flew out of the printer in a fountain of nauseating images. As Tillie texted Jake back to tell him everything was fine and she'd see him tomorrow, she picked up a freshly printed photo of Jake's dad grinning with his chin nestled in Ms. Martinez's beautiful hair. Tossing it onto the desk with all the other pictures from the Mystery of the Missing Father, she thought to herself: *Case closed.*

15

Things Aren't That Simple

WHEN HER ALARM WENT OFF THE NEXT MORNING, Tillie found herself sleeping on the floor with a large spread of photos as her mattress and pillow. Through her window, the sun poured in with a rude, inappropriate brightness. As she lifted herself to wake and rubbed her eyes, she saw that the prints of the door-kiss were crinkled. One of the shots of Ms. Martinez's house had a torn edge. Her photo printer was maxed out. She saw its red light blinking. Her mom would be so mad at how much she'd been printing. "It's more important to pay for printing than to go to college, is it?" she'd say.

The story panned out. She'd gone over it again and again. The lost dad, the cheating husband, the reunion of the glasses with the blind artist. None of it made *sense*, exactly, but it was certain nonetheless; Jake's dad was not on the run, or kidnapped, or a spy, or dead. It was much worse. He was *choosing* to be somewhere else. To be happy somewhere else. He must have been there, at Ms. Martinez's home, the whole time. And Jake's mom must have known. She must have known everything. Jim and Cubicle Man were probably just trying to be good friends, covering for their buddy. Cubicle Man was probably picking up a bag full of Jake's dad's things, handing it off to him so he could go kiss Ms. Martinez. Jake's dad was happily living a life away from his family, causing chaos and sadness all around him without a clue. Or maybe he did have a clue, which made it even worse . . .

How could Jake's parents not tell him this? And did they really think he wasn't freaking out? Did his mom really buy his "I'm fine, I'm fine" act that he was so good at putting on? Even Tillie could see through that!

It was all just too much.

Tillie swept the carpet of photos into a pile. She imagined throwing a match on them and watching them light up into flame. She kicked them under her desk.

"Tillie, are you up?" she heard from the kitchen.

"I'm coming!"

After changing and getting ready for the day, she went to the kitchen only to be greeted by a glum mother. Her dad had left early for work, her mom said. Her mom, looking pale, sipped her coffee and leaned against the sink counter in her robe. She motioned to the toast on the table.

Tillie thought of the night that had just passed. The worry of her mom, the confusion of her dad, the surrender of her parents to not knowing where Tillie had been. She had not taken pictures of whatever argument might have happened between her parents. Her deciphering skills had been focused elsewhere, away from the eternal mystery behind the keyhole.

"Where's Dad?" Tillie asked.

"I told you, at work," her mom said softly.

Her mom took a sip of coffee. Tillie bit into her toast.

"Right, that's just kind of early," Tillie said.

"They needed him in person early this morning to check over some important articles before they went online," her mom said in a voice close to monotone. "Some politician did something awful."

Tillie looked at the clock and saw she was late but did not want to move. First of all, she was still achy. Second, her mother seemed weird.

"So he left that early? For that? Can't they, like, email it to him? Why'd he have to go in to the office?"

Tillie's mom just looked at her.

"Sometimes he's needed, that's all."

Tillie stared down at the cold wads of butter on her bread.

"I know," Tillie responded after a minute.

"What?"

"I know he's needed."

They didn't talk for the next few minutes and then her mom made a "you have to go" face and came over to help her put the backpack on her arms, which Tillie didn't need help with, and hadn't for years, but she didn't have the energy to resist her mom.

As Tillie got to the doorway, she turned back to her mom and asked, "What did the politician do?"

"Hmm?"

"The awful thing he did?"

"Oh, the usual," Tillie's mom said as she turned around to the sink, put her coffee cup down, and began to do the dishes. "He left his wife for some twenty-year-old or something. And then lied about it."

Tillie felt herself unable to move from the doorframe. Maybe she was waiting for a "Don't worry, there are no twenty-year-olds in this town to steal your dad," or even the typical "Be careful today! Did you take your pain medicine?" but there was nothing.

"Okay, bye, Mom." As she was leaving, she added, "I'll be home right away after school."

She saw the back of her mom's head give a nod, and she hobbled off.

Morning math class was a torturous bore. All Tillie could see through the x's and y's on the board was:

BRICK HOUSE + LOST GLASSES = AFFAIR

If "Jake's Dad $+ y =$ Jake's Life as He Knows It Is Over," then y is Ms. Martinez.

In geography, the map of the earth became a map of the neighborhoods in town. If the bowling alley was Africa, then they had been an ocean away from where Jake's dad really was, in North America, which was Ms. Martinez's house. It was a long trip. They'd been so far off. But somehow they were still on the same map, in the same universe. In English, in *Jacob Have I Loved*, Wheeze was Jake's poor mom, and the lucky Caroline was Ms. Martinez. Tillie couldn't listen to a word.

At lunchtime she figured that if she stopped sitting next to Jake's friends then she could be alone again, with no one to hurt or disappoint. And that way, if she told

Jake about where she saw his dad it wouldn't be so bad, because she would be nobody and wouldn't matter. She wouldn't be a girl on the cusp of joining his group as an official friend, and she wouldn't be someone he would then turn to and cry in front of.

But then she saw his face.

"Tillie!" Jake said, beaming.

She had been afraid that seeing him cry would create an awkwardness between them. But instead, as he smiled over at her, she found herself feeling *more* comfortable. She felt like she knew what was behind that smile now. This was a person-to-person knowledge, she realized, that could only be hinted at in photographs. And it felt good to really start to know someone.

She couldn't tell him anything.

"Tillie!" He bounded over to her. "What's up? How's ol' rickety?"

She realized he was referring to her leg and she belly-laughed. No one had ever openly made fun of her leg before, in that way, and it was actually a relief to laugh about it. And a relief to laugh at all.

"It's the usual," she said, working to stifle any more too-loud guffaws.

"Rickety as ever, huh?" Jake asked as he started walking next to her, guiding her toward his lunch crowd. "Sorry about the last two days," he said in a low voice into her ear right as they sat down. "I was in a tight spot with my mom. You sounded like you came up with an idea about the cubicle jerk?"

Tillie shook her head. "No. Nope. I just . . . Well, I thought I did and then I realized it made no sense, so I—"

"Hey, Tillie!" Several voices called out from Jake's table and saved Tillie.

She waved and headed toward them.

He seemed so upbeat. That meant either something was *really* wrong and he was hiding his true state, or he thought he'd found a lead.

"So I went to a rental place yesterday."

"Yeah, you said."

"The one closest to his work. And it was a bust. They wouldn't give me any info. But," Jake continued, "even though they didn't give me any information, it hit me. *Pierce*'s Save-You-Rent Rental Car. Eureka! Why didn't I see it before?"

Tillie stared at him blankly.

"Alice *Pierce*, our classmate," he said. "It's her family. *Pierce*'s Save-You-Rent."

"Okay." Tillie tried to get to the table faster.

"It's her family's rental place! They wouldn't give me info, but Alice could totally help! Maybe get us a look at their actual records and stuff!" He patted Tillie on the back, as if she'd been the one crying at the bus stop. "We're gonna get Cubicle Man. Ya know, in a way it's like what my dad said. He's just a 'blah blah blah' jerk in our ear. And the good guys are gonna get through it."

Tillie said nothing. They sat down at the table with his friends, a little bit removed from them. Tillie tried to look like she was interested in the group's conversation so that Jake would stop talking to her, but Jake went on, anyway.

"So it's totally a thing where my dad saw Cubicle Man do something, right? Because when I said that, he freaked out. So we really have two potential next steps: talk to Alice about the rental car stuff, and go back to my dad's work. I don't know, maybe we find a covert way to sneak into the office this time? I could dress as a delivery boy? Search his cubicle?"

Tillie kept her eyes down, toward her food. "Jake, do twelve-year-olds work as delivery boys?"

Jake smirked. "Stop with the whole overthinking-stuff thing, Hermione. So are you up for it? Look, I know I

191

freaked out, but I'm rested. I'm ready. I'm back in the game."

Tillie had begun to like the "Hermione" nickname. "I told my mom I'd be home today."

The brightness faded from Jake's face momentarily, but then he said, "Okay, sure. But, hey, what about Art Club?"

"What?" Tillie thought of her mom's confrontation about Art Club and for a split second she felt certain that somehow he'd heard her conversation last night, that he'd been following her and taking pictures just as she'd been following his dad. But of course he hadn't heard her or seen her.

"I mean, why don't you just tell her you're going to pretend Art Club again? Twice a week, right?" he said.

"Actually, she knows now that there isn't an Art Club."

"What? How'd she figure it out?"

"Well . . ." Tillie tried to think of how her mom had put it all together. "First of all, I told her I was there, like, multiple days a week and probably in reality school clubs meet only once a week? And I never came home with any art projects, so . . . And then at some point I guess she called the school."

"Oops," Jake said, wincing. "Yeah, we really didn't think through the whole art-projects aspect . . . Nice she notices stuff, though."

Mom-genius wasn't rocket science, actually, Tillie realized. It just involved paying a lot of attention.

"Oh, hey, here's a joke my dad likes to tell that fits us really well: What does a superhero put in his drink?" Jake raised up his plastic water cup in one hand and his pointer finger in the other as if he were giving a superhero lecture.

Tillie sighed. "What, Jake?"

"Just ice." He looked at her expectantly, with a big smile, his huge front teeth on full display. "Just-ice. Get it? Justice!"

"So . . . How exactly does that fit us really well?"

It was Jake's turn to sigh. "Because, silly Tillie, we are looking for *justice*. Like superheroes. For my dad!" Jake shook his head at her with a "tsk-tsk" sound and drank a swig of his water.

"Ah, okay."

They sat in silence, eating their pizza, listening to Ian and Abby debate who would win in a battle, dwarves or elves. And then it was vampires or killer mermaids. When they argued who would win in a fistfight, Snow White or Cinderella, Jake jumped in.

"Okay, obviously it's Snow White. The girl has serious backup."

Tillie realized she had been holding the pizza slice in her hand for a while now and yet she hadn't touched it. She put the slice back down and looked out toward the cafeteria door. The clock above the exit read 12:08. In a few minutes she would have to get up and go to art class. And right next to her, so close that she could feel his jeans graze her own, was a boy whose father that art teacher was hiding. What would Ms. Martinez do if she knew that Jake was crying at bus stops wondering why no one would give him even a hint as to why his dad wasn't home? Did she even care?

Tillie had never kissed a boy, but she knew from the kiss she saw between Jake's dad and Ms. Martinez that it was not the first kiss. It was a familiar kiss. A kiss that people did again and again. A kiss you see in your parents' old wedding pictures. The kiss, and not a coworker, was what had kidnapped Jake's dad.

She couldn't get it out of her mind, the way they had stood there embracing, smiling. All Tillie could think as she had watched them was, *These should not be your smiles. You've stolen Jake's smiles. He deserves to smile, not you.* And all she had been able to do was snap picture after picture as their heads had moved closer together and they had kissed that endless, horrible kiss and shut the door behind themselves.

"So I'll see you soon, okay?" Jake said to her as everyone gathered their stuff to go to their next class. As they stepped away from the crowd, a touch of panic seemed to creep back into his rejuvenated back-at-school self. "It's been two whole weeks now," he said. "Tillie, how worried should I be?"

Tillie felt the words of comfort come out before she could stop herself. "He'll turn up. We'll figure it all out."

The bell rang and everyone started to rush into the halls.

Jake nodded at her with a touch of gratitude. "Okay. And we'll plan a new cover story for your parents, okay? Unless your mom is as good a detective as you are! Then we're really in trouble! Ha!" He trotted off toward class.

"Yeah, okay," she responded to his back.

Charlie Jordan came up to her. He told her he couldn't find a library book he'd taken out and he was going to owe a dollar if he didn't get it back soon. Tillie nodded.

"Thanks, Lost and Found," he said as he broke into a little jog toward class.

"Hey," Tom Wilson said, popping up behind her out of nowhere. "A . . . a note again," he grunted. "Had it yesterday."

Before she could even respond, he'd bolted off.

She was at the stairs, the stairs she regularly felt frustrated by because she couldn't get up to art class fast enough. She usually wanted to get there first, before the rest of the kids, and ask Ms. Martinez questions. But now she just put a single foot on the stairs and felt sick.

So she turned around. She went down the stairs instead of up.

No hall monitors stopped her, as Tillie knew they wouldn't. Spotting her walk, they'd feel too awkward to say anything. The security guard at the front of the school just gave her a compassionate smile and waved to Tillie as she went on her way.

When Tillie arrived at Jake's dad's office she knocked on the glass door to the cubicle area so hard she thought it might break. A lady in a navy-blue pencil skirt opened it. "Can I help you, honey?"

"I'm here on business," Tillie replied as she walked right in, past the woman. People eyed her, but when they saw the limp they turned away. Jake had been a hindrance after all. No one had a reason to look away from him.

When she made it toward the back of the cubicles, she marched toward the man in the last corner cubicle as well as she was able to march. He was typing away. Bored. Going through the motions. She stood at the cubicle's entrance. On the inside corner of the office was a rectangular plaque that read, "Eugene Doyfle." Eugene Doyfle? Cubicle Man was named *Eugene Doyfle*?

"Hi," Tillie said.

Eugene turned and then did a double-take.

"You again," he groaned.

The overhead light reflected off his sweaty, hairless head and produced a slick sheen. She had an artistic urge to take a picture to compare the camera's effect on his features up close to the ones through the glass, but she stopped herself. She left the camera at her chest but did feel her fingers twitching.

"Yup. It's me."

"Kid, I told you . . ."

"I know. 'Don't ask questions you don't want the answers to.'"

Eugene shook his head. "Look, I don't know what you guys want from me. I don't know what your friend thinks about me, but I didn't steal anything, I didn't do anything. You should go."

Tillie couldn't believe she'd ever been scared of this guy. His scar, which had seemed like such a frightening omen to her before, now gave rise to compassion. She imagined he had gotten it in some childhood accident, or something sort of pathetic, like walking into a lamppost.

"You were right," Tillie said.

Eugene raised his eyebrows in a question.

"I didn't want to know the answer."

He rubbed between his eyebrows with his thumb and finger.

"You were covering for Jake's dad," she went on.

He didn't respond.

"Jake's dad told his friends at work that if Jake came by they had to make sure he didn't know his dad was breaking up with his mom. Is that it?" Speaking the words made her understand that they were correct.

"Things aren't that simple," Eugene said, and he stood up, looking around. She saw him catch someone's eye and make a motion with his head that indicated, "Get over here."

Tillie went on. "He knew Jake would come looking for him here, and he told you to cover for him. Was he here the first time we came? Did he see Jake and hide in the back? Or the bathroom?" Tillie said, not waiting for Eugene to answer. "Probably he sent that other guy, *Jim*," she said in a voice dripping with contempt, "to make sure we stayed out. And you watched Jim. You put your finger to your lips to remind him not to break, not to give Jake any hint of the truth."

A couple of people walked by the cubicle and threw quizzical looks in the man's direction.

"You knew he was having an affair."

As she said the words out loud, a calm came over her.

Eugene Doyfle sat back down and put his head in his hand. At his response, any lingering doubts—those parts of her that wanted to be wrong—left her, and she knew she had cracked the case entirely.

"An *affair*," she repeated, as if by saying it twice Eugene Doyfle would better comprehend how horrible it was. "And you were just . . . looking out for your friend. Well, I guess I can't blame you for that."

Maybe Eugene Doyfle was just a good friend. Maybe he was a loyal person who would do anything, even things he didn't like, to help his buddies when they needed him. She'd judged him on his appearance and on the story she'd concocted about him in her head, just like people judged her.

He looked straight at her. "You're Jake's girlfriend or something?"

"No."

With complete defeat he said, "Don't tell him, okay? Don't tell the kid. We promised Dave we wouldn't tell."

Eugene sighed. "How do you worry your kid like that?" he said under his breath.

"He's here now, isn't he?" Tillie moved her head around, looking.

"No, he's not," Eugene answered a little too quickly, grabbing onto the side of his chair like he was ready to bolt.

"He is. Of course he is."

"Just leave it alone, kid, okay? This is grown-up stuff you don't want to get involved in. I tried to warn you. It's a tough situation."

At that moment Jim showed up. He stood at the entrance to the cubicle, and he and Eugene shared a look. Tillie turned to Jim, said, "Please get out of my way," and then moved right past him.

"Hey," she heard Jim say behind her. "Hey, you're limping pretty bad. You hurt yourself? Why aren't you in school? You need a hand? Hey, we'll get you some ice or something. Let's go," he entreated her. "Come on."

"Yeah, I have a limp," Tillie said without turning back to face him. "It's permanent, Jim." She paused and smiled to herself. "Mountain lion attack," she deadpanned as she kept walking, peeking into every cubicle.

Jim followed her, unable to grab a girl with a limp and therefore incapable of stopping her in any way. Behind her she could feel the two men looking at each other, maybe mouthing ideas about what they should do. She became vaguely aware of their voices telling her she had to leave, that it wasn't her place to be doing this.

But then she saw him. The lost dad.

She took in the orange-yellow shine of his hair beneath the overhead lighting. Moving closer, she saw that on the inside of his cubicle he had put up some terrible drawings—one of a man in a wizard hat, one of a stick-figure boy in a cape, and countless others whose scenes were indecipherable—that must have been drawn by Jake.

Jake's dad was on the phone. He held it between his ear and his shoulder. He was speaking in the kind of voice that adults use when they work. Colorless. Tillie stood in his cubicle opening, waiting for him to turn around. When he shifted his eyes a little to see what the presence was behind him, his head froze, but not his mouth. He continued saying "uh-huh, yup, uh-huh" to whoever was on the line. Tillie just looked at him. Up close, she saw, he had more wrinkles than he did in the old pictures Jake had showed her. He had Jake's eyes. Tillie looked right into them.

"I'm missing art class today because of you," Tillie said to Jake's dad. "So thanks a lot."

Jake's dad, still on the phone, all twisted up in his swivel chair, flushed with panic.

"And I'm disappointed in you," Tillie said. He started to say his goodbyes to the person on the other end of the line, and he motioned for her to wait a minute and stay, but before he could hang up, Tillie headed to the elevator.

She did not look back to see what kind of trouble she'd caused.

Tillie headed straight home, and went over and over in her head what she was going to tell Jake, and how.

16

Unavoidable

A CALL WOULD COME FROM THE SCHOOL, IT WAS certain. Someone would report her as having been missing from class. But so far it hadn't happened. An eerie silence filled the house. Tillie had spent so many years wishing her mom would stop talking so much—that she would stop asking if Tillie felt okay, how her leg was feeling, what activities she was doing, reminding her that she could aggravate her leg and her gait could get worse as she got older. Tillie had been so tired, for so long, of saying, "I'm fine," as she watched the other kids do things she couldn't do.

But now she wasn't fine. And no one was asking her if she was or not.

Tillie checked the clock. It was nearly 4 p.m. Time passed so slowly when you got home early.

When her mom returned from work, Tillie heard her footsteps stop by Tillie's bedroom to check for sounds. She shuffled some papers to let her mom know she was there. Moments later, she could hear her mom typing. Her mom always typed like she was angry at her computer. She cooked like that, too. Pots and pans smashing into cupboards.

Tillie did something she rarely did. She put on some music. Bob Dylan. Jake's favorite. She didn't know how she felt about his warbly voice, but she liked the words.

She opened her file drawers and leafed through some old pictures, stopping on one of her dad gazing at the birds, as he often did. He had one of those expressions she had spent so many hours of her life trying to dissect. What was he thinking?

She'd landed on the whole "Dad" file. And this made sense because it took up a huge chunk of her archives. Tillie pulled it out. The file felt thick in her hand. Thicker than she remembered. Her mom was right—she needed to be more selective about what she chose to print. She peeked inside the folder, pulling on the corners of a couple of the photos in there to remind herself of what they were. She caught a glimpse of a picture far in the back. It was from right after she'd gotten the Polaroid camera. She knew this photo well; an old photo was like a favorite song you haven't heard in a while, coming back in a rush.

In the picture, Tillie's dad had a face that looked like he had just seen something tragic on the news. He was sitting on a swing that was ridiculously too small for him. Tillie imagined that she, behind the camera, had probably been giggling. Probably she had hardly noticed his expression, but the camera had captured it.

It had been Parents' Day at school, Tillie remembered, toward the very end of the year, when all the parents come to look at the projects kids have done and watch a performance. She was still recovering from her injuries and surgeries, and hadn't even been in school that spring except for a couple of visits here and there, but she had been desperate to join that day. Her dad had come with her. After sitting in on a few lessons, they'd gone outside to the playground. All the kids had run off in different directions with the groups of friends they always played with. Sydney and Zahreen had probably gone to play mermaids. And Tillie's dad had taken her to the swings. They had tried to find a way for her to swing with his help, but nothing worked. Something about the unsteady movement hurt her back too much. He had told her she should feel free to go play with her friends, but she never played with them anymore, though he didn't know it.

And he'd sat in the swing, and she had taken a picture.

And then, unbeknownst to her, she'd caught that troubled face.

Maybe, Tillie thought, he'd been sad that she couldn't go off to play. He didn't seem to understand that she'd been happy just to be with him.

Tillie put the picture back in the file and felt her phone buzz in her pocket.

"Are you listening to Bob Dylan?" Jake said as she picked up. "I hear it."

"No," she joked, turning the music down. Jake sounded happy, reenergized.

"You like Bob Dylan now. That's awesome."

"What do you want, Jake?" Tillie asked.

"Getting down to business, I like that."

"I'm not going out anywhere, if that's what you're thinking, okay?"

"If there were an Art Club, I'd join it," Jake continued. "Ms. Martinez for an hour after school? Fine by me!"

"You're really annoying, you know that?" Tillie spat out.

"Whoa," Jake said, his voice oddly cheery.

Tillie couldn't take it anymore. Jake tried so hard to prove to the world he was doing okay. There was no way he really felt this good about the Alice Pierce "lead."

"I call it feisty, not annoying. Your greatest strength is also your greatest weakness, and the flip side of being adorable and charming is that you can be a little annoying, too. My mom told me that. Okay, so if we can't go to the Pierces' rental place or Dad's work, I'm just going to come over. Time is moving fast and we gotta get some stuff figured out."

Tillie paused. "Over . . . ?" She stumbled on her words. Where was the "over" he was coming to?

"I think I could get my mom to drive me, actually. Oh, and if your parents want her to come in or something, she's fine about that."

Parents came in when they dropped their kids off? There were so many obnoxious nuances to hanging out with other kids now that she was older. So much had changed since fourth grade. How would she ever learn it all?

"When are you guys having dinner?" he asked.

"What?"

"I can come after."

"Dinner? Well, I can eat whenever, so . . ."

"You guys don't have dinner as a family? Oh, okay. Weird. So then I'll come over ASAP," Jake said. "We can make a plan for the cubicle jerk."

Tillie felt a quick goodbye and then a hang-up coming. She was starting to figure out how Jake worked. Say what you want and then leave before anyone can dispute it.

"No, it's really not a good time," Tillie said. "I mean, there's no point. We can't get anything done here. My mom listens to everything."

"Tillie," Jake said, and there it was: the freaked-out, worried Jake that she knew simmered underneath. "We don't really have a choice. Can you say we're doing homework?" All the optimism dropped from his voice. "My mom has gone so far as to say things to me like maybe next weekend we'll go visit her family in Michigan. She doesn't even seem like she's *trying* to lie to me now, and I don't know what that means. It's like my dad is just *gone*. Also, how did she find out about Pins and Whistles? Maybe she's onto me. Maybe she's trying to get me away from a threat. Look, too much time has gone by since he left. Too much time."

"Fine." Tillie relented.

"We can look at all the photos, huh?" Jake asked. "Look at the timeline?"

Tillie didn't know what to say. "Okay, Jake," she managed.

Jake paused for a minute, as if waiting for her to protest again, and then said, "Great! Bye!"

The photos of Jake's dad and Ms. Martinez still lay in piles on the floor. Tillie collected them and shoved them in a drawer. She pulled out all the pictures that told the fake story, and spread them out on the bed.

Then she went to go tell her mom that Jake was coming over.

When Jake's mom came in, Tillie looked away. If his mom recognized her, Jake would wonder why she hadn't told him she'd gone to his house, and then the whole story would come up, and she hadn't figured out how to explain all of it yet.

The moms introduced themselves, but Tillie saw that her mom was mostly staring at Jake. Jake's mom didn't acknowledge that she knew Tillie at all. It seemed like she didn't even remember her.

His mom looked much more depressed than Jake realized. It was like his mom couldn't see Jake and he couldn't see her.

When they got to her room, Tillie prepped for all

possible embarrassment by just coming out and saying, "She thinks you're my boyfriend."

"Ha! Yeah, Abby's mom thinks I'm hers, too."

"Oh," Tillie said, a little relieved. "Oh, okay."

"You have a minimalist style going on here, Tillie," Jake said, looking around and touching everything. "I'm into it."

"So what was it you wanted to do again?" Tillie asked. "I've got the pictures over here." She stood with her hands in her pockets, pointing her bad foot toward the floor and then flexing it. She tried not to stare at the drawer with the kiss pictures. Her glasses were falling lower down the ridge of her nose than usual, loosened up by a nervous sweat.

Jake sauntered over to the spread.

"Chronological. Cool."

"We have the office photos"—she stuttered on the word "office," thinking of Jake's dad sitting so casually and unperturbed there in that cubicle of his—"and then the car right after. And then Maple Street." They shared a look, remembering the scared girl and the beard and the craziness, and they laughed. "And then there's Pins and Whistles, of course. And"—she sighed—"that's it."

Tillie heard a car leaving their driveway. Jake's mom had left. Now, no matter what, she had to entertain Jake for who knows how long until he decided to get picked up. What did people do when they had someone over? Tillie saw Jake looking down at the pictures on her bed and the kiss flashed through her mind over and over again like someone was flipping the lights on and off. She shook her head, trying to shake the image out.

She couldn't tell him. She just couldn't do it. This would destroy him.

Jake knelt down in front of the bed and picked up each photo as he spoke. "Clearly, whatever trouble Dad is in has to do with these jerks at his job. Otherwise, he never would've left his family. It must be real bad. With friends like these, huh?"

"Yeah, it's strange. Maybe they're not bad, though," Tillie offered. "Maybe it's . . . something else. Something we haven't thought of."

"What do you mean? They're acting all weird about Dad not being at work and then one of them shows up at the place Dad called from and yells at me? And they're not bad?" Jake spoke to Tillie, but his eyes stayed on the picture of him and Cubicle Man—Eugene Doyfle—at Pins and Whistles. It hit Tillie that Eugene must have told Jake's mom about Pins and Whistles, and that was how she'd found out.

"Maybe they're doing something nice," Tillie said. She knelt next to Jake in front of the bed and picked up a picture of the girl screaming on Maple Street. Her eyes were so afraid. The photograph was great, actually, she noticed, with a little pride. "Maybe they're the ones hiding him from the people who really are bad, who made him run away," she suggested.

"I don't think so." Jake dismissed her, moving on to shots further back in their timeline. He scooted around her and went back to the beginning, to the one that started it all—a shot of the office, a shot Tillie had taken just before they went inside. "But I suppose it's possible."

They heard a knock on the door.

Tillie pulled herself up to answer it, opening the door only a crack so that it blocked the bed and all the photos covering it.

It was her mom, peeking through at her. "Could I speak to you alone for a minute?"

Tillie glanced back at Jake, who wasn't even paying attention.

"Sure," she said to her mom, shutting the door behind herself. Her mom started walking toward the kitchen and Tillie followed. Tillie was about to get a be-careful-with-boys talk, she knew it. She should have kept the door partway open or something, but then the photos would be visible to her parents and they would want to see them and would have lots of questions about all the places she'd been sneaking off to recently. Now she had to get a lecture about having friends over, something everyone else did all the time, every day.

"The school called," her mom said, sounding exhausted. "Where were you?"

She had almost forgotten. But she'd been practicing her answer. Tillie was about to say she had had a pain in her back that made her feel claustrophobic at school, and she didn't tell her mom because she didn't want to worry her. But another voice spoke before she could.

"Tillie!" she heard from her bedroom. "Tillie!"

Tillie opened her mouth to speak to her mother, and then looked back to her bedroom door.

"Tillie, what is this?" Jake yelled.

"Tillie, what's going on?" her mom asked sharply, moving closer to Tillie and touching her arm.

Tillie looked toward her mom and back toward the bedroom, then turned her back on her mom and walked away. She opened the door. Jake held a picture in his hand, his face red and pulsing.

"What is this?" he asked, his voice low.

"What?" she said, hoping it was something else, anything but what she knew it was.

What is it? His hand shook and the photo fluttered.

Tillie stepped closer and took the picture from him. She must have missed it when she was picking the photos up earlier. It must have gone flying in the morning when she'd pushed all of them under her desk.

In her hand she held the profile of Ms. Martinez kissing Jake's dad. Their features were clear. Their love was clearer. Looking at it again, Tillie saw how closely their bodies pressed together.

"Tillie, you tell me what this is right now." Jake's voice quivered. But he was not about to cry, like before. He looked like he was about to scream.

"I—" Tillie went to the drawer of her files and pulled out the one with all the pictures from that terrible day. Turning back to Jake, she stayed by the desk and extended her arm, holding out the fateful file. He snatched it from her and sat on the bed, crinkling up all the pictures they already had out.

He pulled the pictures out of their folder and began to flip through them violently. As Jake tore through each one, the series of images went through Tillie's mind in crystal-clear chronological order, like she was watching a movie. Tillie knew that they began at his house, the photos obscured by leaves, and ended with Ms. Martinez in his dad's arms.

When Jake was done, his face had gone from red to white. The pictures lay strewn across his lap, some cascading down to the floor like leaves. Bob Dylan was singing about being tangled up in blue.

"What am I looking at? I don't understand."

The unavoidable truth spilled out. "Your dad is living at Ms. Martinez's house."

Jake took a breath through his nose and his chest rose higher and higher with each inhale. "Why?"

"They're having . . . an affair, Jake."

"But that makes *no* sense." He shook his head. "*No* sense."

"Your mom must have known. She must have not known how to tell you, or—"

"Why was she looking at bank statements then, huh? Why was she . . ." Jake stuttered and couldn't finish.

"I think . . ." Tillie said, trying to be gentle, "I think because they might divorce, maybe? I think that was why?"

"No." Jake stood up. "No, no way. My mom and dad love each other. They're Gimli and Legolas!"

"I know," Tillie said.

"*Everybody fights!*" he said.

"I know."

"*What is going on?*" Jake hollered in a croak.

"I—I don't know, Jake." Tillie reached out to touch him.

Jake slapped her hand away. He paced back and forth a few times and fumed. "Oh, you 'don't know' but you have an entire set of pictures of my dad alive and fine? You 'don't know' but you kept photos of him and . . . *her*," he said with disgust, "in your stupid drawer with your other stupid pictures? You *do* know. You've known. You've known where my dad is. How long, Lost and Found? *How long?*"

"I don't know why any of this is happening! Or how! And don't yell at me!"

Tillie saw her mom's shadow by the door. *Don't come in, Mom*, she thought. *Don't.*

"Why did you keep these to yourself, huh?" Jake asked with a jeer. His face looked cruel, so unlike him. "You just weren't going to tell me? For Christ's sake, you just laid out all our clues but didn't include the ones that led you to *find* him?"

"I don't know what to say." And she didn't.

"Of course you don't. You never do," Jake added under his breath. "I guess that's why you like to be alone."

"Well, maybe it is!" Tillie answered him, standing up

216

straight next to her desk with her hands tightening into fists by her sides.

"I came to you and not my friends because I figured you, out of anybody, would know how to keep a secret. Your whole life is a secret, right? But now you're keeping secrets from *me, too!*" he growled.

"You know what's wrong with you, Jake? You talk so much that you don't hear what other people are saying. How was I even supposed to tell you about what I saw? You are so delusional that you wouldn't have believed your eyes. You would have made up some deranged story about how Ms. Martinez is holding him hostage or something. Well, you know what? She isn't. *You* even love her. So how can you blame your dad?"

"STOP TALKING, TILLIE!" Jake shouted.

"You mean like you never do?" She hated this, hated him.

She saw her mom moving toward the door, as if she might enter. *"Leave me alone, Mom!"* Tillie felt herself howl.

"Well, you know what's wrong with *you*?" Jake leaned toward her with a pointed finger. "You are so *convinced* that something's wrong with you that you thought I wouldn't talk to you anymore if you told me this. Something as important as this. Like there's nothing else about you, except your stupid pictures, that I would like. But guess what, you moron? I *do* like you. You're funny and you're smart and you're kind of weird, and I like that. But why do you have to be such a *liar*?"

"Stop calling my pictures stupid!" Tillie inched closer to his burning-hot face.

Jake laughed a short, bitter laugh. "See? All you care about are these." He gestured at the mess of photos around him. He began to move toward the door, shaking his head in disgust, breathing heavily.

"And you?" Tillie said, and he stopped and turned back to her. "What do you care about, huh? Being the funniest guy around? Making sure everyone thinks you're so great? You know, I saw you in sixth grade, making fun of me. I saw you doing my walk! My limp! Making everyone laugh at me! That's what you care about, huh? Making everybody laugh, no matter who you're hurting!" Tillie was crying now.

"What are you even talking about?" Jake looked at her like she was the delusional one. "I never made fun of you! Not once! Has it ever crossed your insane mind that you're so paranoid that other people are judging you or making fun of you or thinking something bad about you that you thought you saw something you didn't?"

"*I* make stuff up? *I'm* paranoid? You're the one who thought your dad was some hero on the run when really he was just a—" Tillie stopped herself.

"What? What is he?"

Tillie had started sobbing and she couldn't stop.

"Well, you did what I asked," Jake said softly as he turned to leave. "You found him. So thanks, Lost and Found. I guess we're done."

Tillie watched him go, unable to move.

"I didn't want to hide it from you, Jake," she yelled out as he went down the hallway. "I just didn't know what else to do!"

Tillie heard the door slam and hurried toward the window, watching Jake walk away from her house, his silhouette a dot in the night.

Her mom came out from her hiding place outside the door, and held Tillie, weeping, in her arms, telling her it was all going to be alright.

But it wasn't. Because it was the first time she'd ever had a friend over. And it was also going to be the last.

17

Stalker

FRIDAY WENT BY, AND THE WEEKEND, AND TWO more days, and Tillie successfully dodged Jake. She did everything possible to avoid him at school. She waited outside in the mornings until the majority of kids had entered the building, arriving a little late to her class, just so she wouldn't see him before first hour. She took alternate routes to her classes to make sure she didn't pass his locker. She ate lunch in the math teacher's room, where kids were welcome if they wanted to do homework. She scribbled random numbers into her notebook.

And then, on Wednesday at lunchtime, Abby stopped her in the hall.

"Where have you been?" she asked. "Come eat with us."

Before Tillie could protest, Abby added, "And hey, is Jake okay? Seriously. He's been at your old table all week."

Really? She could hardly imagine it.

"Oh," Tillie said. "I actually really don't know."

Abby shrugged. "Okay." She linked her arm through Tillie's and walked her toward the cafeteria.

As Tillie made her way into the lunchroom with Abby, she saw Jake seated where she used to sit, slouched over his tray, headphones on. She didn't have to worry about catching his eye because his focus stayed entirely downward.

When they joined the group at the table, Abby started asking Tillie about when she got into photography. As Tillie haltingly began to tell the story about her grandpa and the Polaroids she heard someone say "Jake" from a little ways down the table. Tillie paused to listen.

"He's over there at the Lost and Found table," she heard Ian say.

"Yeah, is he the new Lost and Found or something?" Emma said.

"Maybe he'll come in tomorrow lugging a weird old camera," Ian said.

The group of them laughed.

Abby turned to Tillie, and then back to her crowd. "She's right here, guys! Can we get a little respect?"

"Oh, hey, Tillie," Ian said. "We were just messing around. No hurt feelings, right?"

Tillie ate her grapes and meatloaf in silence. She couldn't escape to her old table because it wasn't hers anymore. Her cafeteria hideout had been stolen.

Abby leaned in to whisper in her ear. "News flash— Ian is kind of a jerk." She nudged Tillie's shoulder and smiled. Tillie did her best to smile back.

She tried to ignore Jake, even though he was all she could think about.

She promised herself she would never eat lunch in the cafeteria again.

In Tillie's first art class since her fight with Jake, Ms. Martinez talked them through a watercolor of an orange and an apple. "Use a thick brush to create the background space, covering your canvas. Use a small brush to add detail. Pay attention to the light. Don't be afraid to mess up. Colors are malleable."

The fruit bowl sat in the center of the room and the kids worked on stained wooden easels the school must have been using for two decades.

Tillie fantasized about spending the class pretending

to draw the apple and orange and then when they turned their easels around to show what they'd done, she would reveal a painting of Ms. Martinez kissing Jake's dad.

As Ms. Martinez walked past Tillie's canvas she said, "Good job." But it was like an outline of "Good job," with none of the color it usually had.

Tillie forced herself to look up at Ms. Martinez and act like everything was normal.

"Thanks," she started to say, but as she took in Ms. Martinez's face, she stopped. Ms. Martinez's eyes were glued on her, as if she'd just been waiting for the chance to share one small, private glance, and her expression told Tillie that she knew everything. Her brow furrowed, not in anger, but in an awful mixture of sadness and disappointment. She pointed toward her glasses and said, "Got them back," in a low, deliberate voice. Then she shook her head slightly, as if shooing away some unpleasant thought, and moved on to the next student's work.

So she knew what Tillie had seen. Who else knew? Had Jake confronted his parents? Had Jake's dad told Ms. Martinez about the girl at his office? It didn't really matter. It was done.

When the bell rang, Tillie rushed out of the room without looking at Ms. Martinez's face.

Her dad—never home right after school—was in her room. Waiting for her.

He sat on her bed, surrounded by pictures.

"Matilda . . ." he said when she opened the door. He didn't look at her. His eyes were fixed on the images before him, toppling over his thighs and onto the bed. Some were on the floor.

She wanted to say, "Whatever the teacher or grown-up who called you said is wrong. I didn't do anything, I was just trying to help someone." But she didn't. She couldn't. All she managed to say was, "Why aren't you at work? Where's Mom?"

Tillie's dad didn't respond.

And then another possibility occurred to her. Maybe, after all this time, he had discovered her photos' worth, their beauty. Maybe he wasn't mad about the search for Jake's dad. Maybe he was too awed to speak.

"I find things for people, with my camera." She'd always wanted to tell him this. "They call me Lost and Found." She nodded toward the puddle of photographs.

She forced a small laugh, as if to signal it was no big deal. At the same time, she checked his face to see if there was any reaction. But he remained blank.

224

So she stood still and waited. Her leg was starting to hurt from standing in one place for too long. Her dad picked up a picture and then put it back down.

"Dad . . ." She came toward him to sit on the bed.

But before she got there, her dad lifted up a picture. He stared right at her, with a tight mouth and a locked jaw. He turned the image toward Tillie. Her dad held a picture of himself, with a tiny flash of her mom's cheek. It was a photo she'd taken through the keyhole in their bedroom door. A close-up of his face. In the photograph his face was absent of feeling in that way a face gets when a person becomes overwhelmed and needs to just shut down. It was a photo Tillie had spent a lot of time looking at, wondering if he was thinking of her and her leg, or her mom, or something else— some mysterious something else that made him so un-knowable.

She looked at the photograph and then back at him.

"What is this?"

"A picture," Tillie whispered.

There was a long pause.

"What is the *meaning* of this?"

"You know I use my camera a lot," Tillie said, trying to make her voice light. She wished she could say, "You know I love my camera more than anything."

"You've been looking at your mom and me? When we're in private?"

She couldn't speak.

Her dad stood up and began to pace. His voice, which rarely held much expression in it at all, boomed and filled the room.

"Your mom made me come in here. To see what might be true about a call from that boy's mother."

So Jake had told his mother he knew. His mother had told his dad. His dad had told Ms. Martinez about the office showdown and with the details from Jake's mom she must have put it all together. Tillie cursed Jake in her head.

"And this is what I find," he went on. "Me and your mother." He paused and stopped in place, shaking his head at all that lay before him. "And so much of me . . ." He bent and sifted through some pictures on the bed. Tillie saw that it was the "Dad" file.

"Talk about invading privacy," Tillie said under her breath.

"So I'll ask you again. What is the meaning of this?"

Tillie tried to remember the last time he'd been in her room this long.

"I love to take pictures." Tillie's voice shook. The pain in her back and leg had tripled since the morning. "Like

Vivian Maier. I Googled her, Dad." Tillie paused, waiting for something, anything. "I could be as good as her one day," she added desperately.

Tillie's dad looked her up and down. "I can't believe this." He put his hand to his head. "You're nearly thirteen years old, and all you do is watch other people. Like a . . . a *stalker*."

Tillie's mouth parted, but no sound came out.

"I'm so sorry, Tillie. I'm so sorry for what I did to you," he said. He started to walk out of the room, but he stopped when he was next to her and said, "But this has to stop. No more camera. No more pictures. Nothing. You're not okay."

18

Break

SHE KNEW HOW TO SNEAK OUT NOW. NO PROBLEM
at all. But holding four cameras was a challenge.

Outside she felt a slight end-of-March drizzle. Spring
was so close, but the air remained cold and dreary. In
her front yard she spotted a few buds. She stepped on
them as she walked across the lawn to the garbage.

The trash bins sat by the curb. Tillie put the cameras
down next to them.

She grabbed her tiny range finder first. It was easy to
break. She just held it, said her goodbyes, and threw it
down onto the road. It cracked on the concrete, and with
one stomp from her good leg, she turned it into a piece
of trash.

This would make everybody happy. No more "stalking," no more ruining lives.

Her huge film camera, the one that used to be her mom's, the one that her Google research told her was the same kind of medium-format film camera Vivian Maier used to secretly capture people's lives on the streets of Chicago, would be more difficult to destroy. Tillie lifted it above her head with both hands.

Art should capture something true, Ms. Martinez had said. But Ms. Martinez had just been a big lie.

With a grunt, Tillie hurled the camera onto the cement as hard as she could.

No one *wants* the real truth. Jake hadn't wanted to see that he was just another sad kid from a broken family. And she hadn't wanted to see that she was just a broken girl. But he *was* sad, and she *was* broken.

The lens cracked into a dozen shards, but only a tiny section of the camera's body came off, and Tillie cursed.

It wasn't her body that was the broken part. No. It was *her*. She was awkward. A lurker, a *freak*. Was that because she was in pain nearly all the time? Was that because people either stared at her or looked away as fast as they could when she walked down the street? Maybe. But it didn't really matter why.

"Come on," she said aloud. "Break." She kicked the camera with her good leg.

Except that it mattered to her mom, who didn't let her go a second without reminding her that she was different, that she was alone.

"Break!" she commanded with another kick.

And it mattered to her dad. The "why" meant *everything* to her dad.

Tillie took the metal top off the trash can and held it up high.

I'm so sorry for what I did to you . . . he'd said.

Tillie brought the trash can lid down onto the camera with a loud crash. The camera splintered into pieces.

Next, Tillie grabbed her best friend, her beautiful DSLR, the one that had captured most of her Lost and Found shots, and placed it by the scraps of metal and glass that lay before her. She lifted the lid again.

Oh, yeah? You're sorry, Dad?

She brought it down. A couple of fragments of the camera flew off the curb and onto the street's pavement.

Then why did he just ignore her*?*

She bashed it again. Harder.

So they got into an accident! He hurt her! By *accident*! Because of *bad luck*! Okay, fine!

She smashed it harder.

Did that mean he had to stop laughing and smiling? Did that mean he had to stutter and mope and *be ashamed of her*? And anyway, he hadn't *done anything to her*! This all had nothing to do with him! She would've found and loved photographs no matter *what* happened to her, no matter *what* path she'd taken. It was *who she was*!

But not anymore.

Tillie slammed the lid down on the remains of her Lost and Found camera again.

No more "stalker."

And again.

No more freak.

And again.

Three cameras lay decimated before her. Garbage.

The last camera to destroy was the Polaroid camera her grandpa had given her, the one that no longer worked. It would fall apart with one strike, she knew, but she couldn't do it herself. She pressed it to her cheek, and placed it in the middle of the road. The next car that came would do the dirty work for her.

She looked out at the mess she'd created. A picture *did* say a thousand words, Tillie thought. And her pictures had been her screams, showing the world that she was on the outside of it. She only watched, lived in life's periphery, told other people's stories . . . And now, without her photos, she'd just be silent.

Sweeping up the other cameras' remains, she put them into the trash bit by bit, and that was that. As she walked back into the house, she heard a car drive by and the Polaroid camera crumple beneath it.

There you go, Dad, thought Tillie. *No more cameras.*

19

Drawing with Light

"AND SO 'PHOTO' MEANS LIGHT. AND 'GRAPH' means drawing or writing. So, therefore, 'photography' means drawing with light. If you think about it, it's pretty interesting. Because we think of photography as just something our parents do to make sure they remember us when we were babies, but really it's a science and an art about light and how it reflects in the world."

Tillie had written the assignment, an essay on "What I Love" in the autobiography unit in her English class, begrudgingly. It had been three weeks since she'd given up photography, and it seemed so stupid to still talk about it, but she didn't know enough about anything else.

She felt nauseated up there, giving a speech. Presenting

in class was the worst. In the back of the classroom, people giggled, so she spoke as fast as she could.

"They used to say that photographs captured people's souls." She had to go faster, the laughter was getting louder. "But even though that's obviously not true, people were very superstitious back then. People were scared of it. Since its invention, photography has struggled to be respected, but now it has finally been accepted as an art form. Thankyouverymuch."

She sat down.

Everyone was still laughing. Possibly it wasn't at her, but it felt like it was. She recalled Jake saying, *You're so paranoid that other people are judging you . . . You thought you saw something you didn't . . .* Maybe he was right.

After English class, Diana Farr, flanked on either side by two of her usual sidekicks, stopped her in the hall.

"Great speech," Diana said, and the two girls snickered.

"Um, thanks," Tillie said, keeping her head down.

"So why'd you try and ruin my life?" Diana said next, jolting Tillie into looking up into her eyes.

"Um, what?"

Diana's arms crossed. Her hip jutted out to one side.

"You told me Joaquin liked me," Diana said.

"He does," Tillie maintained.

"He *doesn't*!" Diana snapped. "I've been waiting for him to ask me out for *a month*! I've turned down Ian and Ahmed *and* Christian! And then I finally text him last night, saying, 'What's the deal? I like you a lot, obviously,' and he goes, *'You're awesome and pretty, but I don't know how you got that impression. I like someone else.'"* Diana grimaced. "Someone else . . ."

"The pictures made it look like he liked you!" Tillie stammered. "He kept . . . staring at you!" Maybe he'd just been staring at her like everyone stared at her, Tillie realized. Maybe it was nothing special for him, and maybe, once again, Tillie knew nothing about other people at all.

"Well, you were *wrong*," Diana said. She put a hand up as if to shush Tillie, though Tillie hadn't said anything more. "Stop messing with my life. Just stay away from me."

"Yeah," her two sidekicks parroted.

And with that, Diana Farr and her friends strutted off.

"You *asked* me to mess with your life!" Tillie yelled after them, though they were too far away to hear her.

Tillie took a breath and put her hand to her chest to touch her camera, but it wasn't there. What a shame. Diana's perfectly highlighted hair would have made a great subject for a photograph as it swayed down the hall.

Without the constant promotion of Diana Farr, and certainly without her cameras, her life as the Lost and Found would officially be over. Tillie tried to muster up a feeling of loss about this, or indignation, or something, but, to her surprise, she just felt numb. It was a relief to go back to being no one. After everything that had happened, it would be nice to disappear again entirely. Besides, she didn't have any cameras left, anyway.

"Hey, Lost and Found!" someone said as Tillie walked, head down, toward her locker.

Tillie didn't answer.

"Hey!" There was a moment's pause. "Hey!"

Tillie recognized the voice of Tom Wilson, whose love note she'd found. Had it been just a few weeks ago? It felt like a lifetime.

Tillie kept walking, determined to get away from what would surely be one of the last calls for the Lost and Found.

Tillie had spent the past three weeks, most of April, avoiding Jake and re-creating her previous existence as a middle-school hermit. It helped that her parents had grounded her, which meant she had to come home right after school. They took away her cell phone and gave her

Dad's old pager. "It's from the days of antiquity," her dad said. "It's for emergencies," her mom insisted. Every time Abby saw her she tried to get Tillie to come to lunch with her, and even asked a couple of times why she hadn't texted her back, and Tillie told her she was in trouble for getting bad grades in math, so she had to make sure to work on homework every day. One day Abby asked her why she didn't have her camera anymore, and Tillie said, "Actually, my favorite one broke, so . . ." and she felt like she might cry, so she turned on her heel and sped off as best she could. This humiliating interaction made her want to escape Abby, and all other human beings, even more.

A couple of times, as she went from her lunch in the math room toward art class, she thought she heard Jake's voice, and she hid inside the nearest girls' bathroom until there was no way he could still be around.

Ms. Martinez had spent the last three weeks acting like nothing had happened. She complimented Tillie's work and smiled at her. She didn't offer her any winks, it was true, but she also didn't give her disappointed gazes.

And then, one afternoon, Ms. Martinez announced who she had chosen to be featured in the school art show that year: Deshaun Washington. Matt Ross. Tillie Green.

Deshaun and Matt bumped chests and did a boy-hug. Tillie looked away from Ms. Martinez.

"Congratulations, guys." Ms. Martinez beamed as the class applauded half-heartedly.

She showed them Deshaun's clay sculpture of a turtle, Matt's collage self-portrait, and a photograph of Tillie's dad. In it, her dad bent over a plate of uneaten mashed potatoes, reading a newspaper, and behind him in the reflection of the kitchen window's glass was Tillie with her camera, focused directly on him. It was the kind of photo that Tillie thought of as a "trick"—it only looks cool, when really it's clichéd and has been done a million times. But the lighting in the shot was good, and she had been proud enough of it to turn it in for one of their "free subject" assignments.

"No," Tillie said.

The class quieted.

"I mean, no thanks," she amended.

"Oh, Tillie, but it's an honor! We hang them in the hallway, parents come, and then they're up for a day or two."

"No, it's okay," Tillie said. "No thanks."

Ms. Martinez gave her a long stare. Then she raised her voice and said, "Who thinks Tillie's photo should go in the art show? Come on, guys!" Her forced peppiness reminded Tillie of her mom, and Tillie grimaced.

A couple of unexcited "woo"s could be heard, and other than that it was silent.

"Okay." Ms. Martinez surrendered, her eyes lingering on Tillie for a moment, and moved on.

Leaving school and heading toward the bus, Tillie saw a familiar face in the line of cars waiting to pick up kids. Jake's dad sat there, tapping on his cell phone, looking up every once in a while, probably to see if his son or maybe his girlfriend was among the throngs of people rushing out. After a few minutes, Jake appeared and jumped into the front seat. His dad said something and Jake laughed. Maybe he'd told him one of his classic dad jokes, Tillie thought. Jake opened the window a little bit and hollered something to a group of older kids. The kids laughed, and Jake's dad laughed, too. For a brief moment, Tillie thought she saw the smile wipe off of Jake's face and then paste back on again, but she couldn't be sure. Father and son drove away together, and Tillie shuffled off to the bus.

20

Into the World

HER PARENTS THOUGHT GROUNDING TILLIE WAS a real punishment. They hadn't figured out yet that the "boyfriend" they were so worried about was really a fluke friend. Her mom kept saying things to her like, "You know, if you'd used your time and talents more wisely, maybe you'd have time to spend with your boyfriend." Jake would have found that really funny.

Tillie spent her days watching lots of TV. The mystery shows her parents watched seemed ridiculous to her now. They always ended with some satisfying, good-over-evil resolution. It was unrealistic. Tillie did her PT exercises like clockwork. She finished all her chores each week, and completed her homework right on time. She pretended to listen when her parents had talks with her about affairs and assured her they wouldn't ever divorce. She just smiled and nodded. She acted like a model kid. A bored-out-of-her-mind, model kid.

On a Saturday, as she put away the dishes from lunch, her dad, working on his laptop at the kitchen table, picked up his phone. After answering, his voice lowered and Tillie turned to see her mom mouth, *Who is it?* He got up and went to continue the call in the bedroom as her mom followed.

A few minutes later, they came back in together and stood at the kitchen table.

"Hey, honey?" said her mom.

When Tillie turned around she saw they wore serious, we-have-to-talk expressions. What other secrets of hers had they discovered? Did they realize she'd snuck out once? Did they uncover more pictures of themselves on her laptop?

"Honey, Ms. Martinez just called."

Tillie wiped her hands on her jeans and turned to them, leaning against the sink. "Okay . . ."

"She told your dad that you've been chosen to be in the school art show?"

Tillie sighed. "Oh. That. Yeah, I was, but it's not a big deal." She turned back to the sink.

"Sweetheart, come here, okay?" her mom asked, and Tillie begrudgingly came, and they all sat down.

Tillie started playing with a paper napkin on the table, picking it apart into little strips.

"She said you said no," her dad said in a near-whisper.

"Yeah. It's just not a great picture."

"She told your dad you're really talented." Her mom reached out across the table. Tillie dropped the napkin and let her mom grab her hand. "That it wasn't even a question of whether or not you'd be chosen."

Tillie couldn't imagine it hadn't been a question. Not after what had happened. But would Ms. Martinez call her parents and say that if she didn't mean it?

"She told your dad she's not supposed to say this," her mom continued, "but your work is her favorite, no question, and she said we should try to convince you to let your work go in. She said it's an honor. It's just three kids in each grade, Tillie."

Was this Ms. Martinez forgiving her? Was this her peace offering?

"Look, we know she hurt you. And trust me, we don't approve of her actions in that situation."

Tillie knew. They'd explained to her that Ms. Martinez and Jake's dad had done something wrong, but they'd emphasized over and over that "marriage is complicated."

"But she's still your teacher," her mom continued, "and this is still a . . . a special thing. You can let it be about your accomplishments. Not her . . ."—her mom paused and inhaled deeply—"mistakes."

"I'll think about it," Tillie said.

Her mom squeezed her hand. "Thanks, sweetie."

Tillie got up, left the last dishes for later, and went toward her room.

Her dad stopped her in the hallway.

"Tillie," he said, slowly, as if he was about to impart something very important.

Tillie looked up at him. His eyes fell to their typical resting place at his feet.

"Tillie, she said your art . . . captures something true." He looked like he wanted to say something else, but, as usual, didn't.

"Okay, Dad," Tillie said. "I really will think about it."

He nodded and went back toward the kitchen.

Tillie sat by her windowsill, watching the occasional passerby and the swooping birds. She could only imagine

the murmurs that would fill her parents' room that afternoon.

She said your art captures something true.

Tillie remembered how Ms. Martinez had said that
same thing to her in the car the day she'd driven Tillie
to the doctor's. *Art should capture something true, you know?*
she'd said. *And your photos do that.*

Tillie could perfectly picture that memory of Ms.
Martinez, her mind's eye's image of the woman from
two months ago who kindly picked her up from the
bus stop. Someone who had told her she should feel free
to make mistakes on an art project, but who Tillie as-
sumed never made any mistakes herself. Tillie hadn't
truly known her then, and, really, she *still* didn't know
anything about Ms. Martinez. She knew one day, one
part of a story. But she'd never known Ms. Martinez's
reasons, her feelings, her truth. So she could hate the
Ms. Martinez that now existed in her head. Or maybe
she could just . . . forgive her, like Ms. Martinez seemed
to be forgiving Tillie. She could just let her be a *different*
Ms. Martinez now.

Tillie could also vividly picture herself that day—the
girl who'd been in the passenger's seat. That girl was different, too. Back then, Tillie had been scared of everyone. She'd let her pictures speak for her, but she never

truly spoke for herself. She'd simply run errands for other kids, happy for a peek into other lives that seemed more full. But now she had stepped into her own life. She'd stepped into the *world*, walked through the Illinois night, followed leads to bowling alleys, sung and danced in front of strangers, and confronted a man who had once terrified her.

And so much of that was because of the time she'd spent with Jake.

It was because Jake had *seen* her. When he looked at her he didn't only see how she walked. He even seemed to *like* how she walked, like it made her . . . herself. And it did. It was a part of her. He didn't see a weirdo behind a camera. He saw a detective, an artist. And she was those things. She always had been. In some part of herself, she'd known that for a long time.

But Jake had also seen someone he could trust, and she hadn't been that person. She'd broken that trust.

She had to apologize to Jake. She had to say she was sorry, right away. She'd avoided him, she'd given up on the idea of him, but maybe if Ms. Martinez could still care about Tillie enough to call her parents even with all that had happened and gone unspoken between them, then maybe Jake could still care about her, too, and forgive her, even though she'd hurt him.

Just the thought of it flooded Tillie with relief.

Tillie bounded toward her parents' room.

"Is everything okay, honey?" her mom asked.

"Yeah," Tillie said. "I have to go out, though."

"No," her mom said. "Absolutely not."

"It's just really important."

"I'm not going to allow that, Miss Tillie."

"Mom," she implored. "I have to go talk to Jake. I have to tell him I'm sorry, okay? About everything that happened."

"Oh," her mom said, taken aback.

"I need to apologize," Tillie said.

"I see, honey," her mom said with a smile. She made a motion with her hands as if scooting Tillie out of the room. "Yes, okay, go. Go."

"Yes, go," her dad piped in. "Good," he added quietly as Tillie put her shoes on.

Her mom got up to grab her purse and car keys. "I'll drop you off," she said. "And I'll pick you up a half hour later, okay?" She held out Tillie's phone. "I'll call you when I'm on my way. But you're still grounded."

Tillie barely heard her. She was already out the door.

21

The Truth

JAKE OPENED THE DOOR TO HIS HOUSE. HE DIDN'T seem surprised to see her.

He shut the door behind him, and came out to her on the porch, leaning against the outside of the house.

"Is your mom okay?" Tillie asked, despite what she already knew.

"I guess she will be," Jake said. He paused and then added, "They're getting divorced. He'll probably continue to stay with Ms. Martinez for now. I think."

Tillie knelt down to his front step to sit. He joined her.

"It's nice out." Tillie looked up at the green trees.

"Yeah," he said.

"I'm sorry . . ." she began.

But before she'd even finished her words, Jake chimed in. "Don't be."

"I didn't—" she started.

"Why didn't you call me back?" Jake asked.

"Huh?"

"I called you and texted you a bunch. I mean, not at first, but after, like, a week. I tried to catch you a couple times. I called your name once or twice and you ran into the bathroom," he said. "Abby said she tried to reach you a lot, too. She asked me about you. She thinks you're awesome."

"Really?" Tillie couldn't quite believe it. "My mom took my phone. And I guess I just . . . didn't want to see anyone. Didn't want to be seen."

"Well, anyway. You're here." Jake had bags under his eyes. Even though from afar she'd watched him laughing with his dad, probably trying to pretend he was okay, she bet he'd done some more crying, too.

"Right after all that happened," he said, "my dad told me how you came to see him. How you yelled at him and those guys." Jake shook his head in disbelief. "That's pretty awesome."

"I told Jim I got my limp from a mountain lion attack."

Jake snorted, looking like his old self again for a moment. "Oh my God. You're serious?"

Tillie nodded.

"Oh, that's brilliant. Ya know, we need to think of other answers you can give people when they ask. You survived an avalanche! Or you fought off a killer octopus or something. Ha!"

She smiled. "Yeah . . . Not bad ideas, but I think I need to stick to the truth from now on."

"Yeah . . . The truth," Jake said to no one in particular.

"Well, anyway . . ." Tillie went on, "I should have told you about your dad right away and I'm sorry, I'm really sorry." She said this quickly so he couldn't cut her off. She had to say it.

Jake didn't respond.

"You know, it's so weird here," he said after a moment. "My dad comes, picks me up, takes me to lunch. Tells me how great 'Chrissy' is."

"Chrissy?"

"Oh, yeah. Ms. Martinez has a cheerleader name."

"Wow."

"And then I come home, and my mom is asking me what he said, and it's all just . . . It's just pretty weird."

"I'm really sorry," Tillie said.

Jake paused again, looking up at the sky. "I was so angry at him." With his elbows resting on his knees, he began softly punching one hand into the other, cracking his knuckles. "That first time I saw him, he sat me down. Told me how he'd met 'Chrissy' at our stupid parent-teacher conferences last spring when I first took art, how they became 'best friends.' Told me how he couldn't help what he felt with her . . . You should have seen me, Tillie. He told me he could take it, that he could take anything I had to say to him and that he'd deserve it. At first, I said to him, 'I thought *I* was your best friend,' which seemed to hurt him. Which was *good*. And then, I just told him I didn't understand why he would go off and disappear like that, for *any* reason. Why he wouldn't tell me where he was or what was going on. He said . . ." Jake bit his lip. "He said he couldn't face me."

Jake told Tillie that his parents had made a deal: since Jake's dad had cheated, he would be the one to leave, and he would be the one to tell Jake.

"Your mom made up the work-vacation lie to stall for him," Tillie jumped in, putting the final pieces together.

"Yup," Jake said with a tight, stern mouth.

His parents kept making plans for when Jake's dad would tell Jake, and then his dad would put it off. Jake's performance at home convinced his mom he was completely innocent of the situation, and so she just kept waiting for his dad to get the courage to confess. Out of anger, Jake's mom took his dad off the family phone plan, which was why Jake couldn't reach him.

"That's why he called from a blocked number. You think he blocked the number of the call from Ms. Martinez's phone?" Tillie asked.

Jake signaled "yes" with a single nod.

"And when he called from Pins and Whistles you finally saw a number."

"I guess he had more bravery that night." Jake continued to crack his knuckles.

Since the family only had one car, his dad rented one for himself—a blue Chevy Malibu. He drove along Jake's route to school a couple of times, hoping he'd get some courage. After Jake had shown up at his work with Tillie, his dad hid from him, but then jumped in the car, determined to tell him, only to lose his nerve again when he saw Jake. Just as Tillie had suspected, Jake's dad's coworkers knew the whole situation, and they had tried to keep Jake away until his dad could handle telling him.

"Basically, my dad's a huge coward." Jake gazed out toward the street and the sky. "Why wasn't *someone* just straight with me? Divorce sucks." He put his head in his hands. "And how do I know the lies have stopped? For all I know, he was actually driving toward the school each morning to see 'Chrissy,' *not* to try and tell me. Ya know what? He's not just a coward. He's a jerk," Jake said with a touch of venom, lifting his head up. He squinted in the sunlight and, without his usual wide-eyed expression, he looked much, much older.

Tillie didn't want to call Jake's dad a jerk, even though Jake had admitted it already and even though she agreed with him, so she remained quiet.

"But he's still my dad," Jake added, as if he'd heard her thoughts. "And my mom's still my mom."

They sat in silence and watched the sights before them: the sycamore tree and the forsythia bush in the corner of the yard, the parents strolling by with their little kids, headed to the park for a sweet, sunny Saturday.

"Why are adults so stupid?" she said finally.

"I do *not* know," he answered.

A neighborhood cat scrambled by, and a toddler chased it, giggling, stumbling.

"I feel like my dad has been missing for four years," Tillie said, feeling the words rush out like a wave.

"What do you mean? Your parents aren't divorced," Jake said.

"You want to know how my leg really got messed up?" Tillie asked.

Jake nodded.

"I used to be able to walk perfectly," Tillie said. "And no pain."

Jake leaned in toward her. "What happened?" he asked faintly.

"My dad . . ." She tried to speak and had to stop and start twice before it came out. "My dad was being funny. We were in the car. I remember laughing a lot because he was so funny. He was going really fast. That's what I was told afterward. I . . ." She struggled to put it all together, to really remember. "I don't think even *so* fast, but still, just a little too fast for the weather, because we were late, and my parents both hated being late. They still do."

She no longer saw the pavement ahead of her or the jeans on her legs or Jake sitting next to her. She saw the snowy trees out the car window. "And we were going to see my grandpa. Grandpa was turning sixty or seventy-something . . . sixty. Yeah, sixty. And it was just one of those Illinois winter days . . . There was snow, it was icy, and we were just . . . going too fast. We were just joking and laughing and in a hurry and we didn't slow down enough. Or not 'we.' *Him. He* didn't slow down enough. And when we hit an ice patch we spun and spun," she said, and just saying the word made her feel dizzy, as if she were in the car again, spinning and spinning and spinning, "and we slammed right into a tree and . . ."

She saw the slice of black metal as it slammed against her torso. She heard the click her back made when it fractured, and the cry she had let out, and an old memory hit her. Her dad had cried out at exactly the same time.

"My hip shattered. My back fractured. I broke three ribs."

"Oh my God," Jake said.

"I know, right?" Tillie shook her head, incredulous at her own story. "I broke a hip! An eight-year-old! Oh, and my pinky toe broke, too," she added. "Can't forget that one."

"Yeah, don't leave out poor Pinky," Jake said.

She tilted her chin toward him, but still couldn't look at him. "And even when the bones healed," she continued, "somehow things never stopped . . . hurting."

"Man," said Jake. "I'm . . ." And it sounded like he was going to say, "I'm sorry," but thought better of it. "So did your dad get hurt, too? Is that why he's . . . 'missing'?"

"No. He's . . . not missing like that . . . Like, he's just not *there*. He just couldn't get over it . . ." Only as Tillie said all this out loud, finally, did she understand how true it was. "He felt really bad, my mom used to say, back when I used to ask. I guess I don't remember him much before the accident, anyway, only in these fuzzy memories I wonder if I made up . . . So maybe he was always . . . I don't know. He just can't look at me. That's what it is. He doesn't look at me. Not for more than a second or two at a time. He feels too bad that I can't play soccer— he *loves* soccer—or make friends easily, like people might think I'm freakish or not get all I have to deal with, and he feels bad because he thinks I'm weird, I guess. And since he doesn't look, he doesn't know I'm actually fine! He doesn't know me at all." Tillie looked up and met Jake's eyes.

"Well . . . That's too bad for him, then," Jake said.

Her phone vibrated on the porch's cement. They watched it light up and then stop.

"Mom's on her way," she said to him.

"So, were you mad at him? Are you?" Jake asked, his face ever-curious.

Tillie paused. "Not mad about the accident. Just the not-getting-over-it part, I guess."

"Does he *think* you're mad about the accident?"

She paused again. Did he?

"I don't know," she said, picturing her dad's face in a hundred photographs. Stricken. Definitely guilty. But was he afraid she was *mad*? It didn't seem possible.

"Ya know, there's something I never told you." Jake interrupted her thoughts.

Tillie looked at him.

"About my dad leaving."

She nodded for him to go on.

"A couple days before he disappeared, he and my mom got into this massive fight." He paused, eyeing her reaction, and then went on. "I mean, they were *really screaming* at each other. Saying . . . well, really mean stuff." He took a breath. "I should have known why he was gone."

"Maybe you kinda did." Tillie shrugged.

Tillie pictured how scary it would be if her parents screamed and didn't just whisper harshly when they thought she wasn't looking.

"Ya know," Jake said, "I'm really sad my dad lied to me. But I really don't think my mom was very happy. I don't think either of them were." He sighed. "Are you mad? That I hid a big clue from you?" he asked.

Tillie shook her head hard. "No. Definitely not."

"Thanks," he said.

They both looked out at the front yard again. A dozen birds flew through the sky and landed on a telephone line across the street.

"Hey, Tillie?" Jake said.

"Yeah?"

"One more thing."

"Oh, no . . ." Tillie said, laughing a little. "What is it now?"

"No, seriously, I have to say this. Ya know how you said you thought you saw me making fun of you?" Jake bit his lip.

"Yeah, I'm sorry, I just—"

"The truth is,"—Jake interrupted, holding his hand up to quiet her—"maybe I did." He looked right at Tillie, contrite. "I honestly don't remember. And I'd like to think I didn't, that I wouldn't do that, but I don't know. Last year? I was nervous, like, at all times. I did stupid stuff. I *do* stupid stuff."

"We all do stupid stuff," she said.

"You got that right. Well, thanks."

They both put their legs out straight as they sat on the front step, and leaned into each other so that they were shoulder-to-shoulder, looking out. They sat together for a while, watching the nice day roll by, until her mom pulled up to the curb. Jake stood and offered a hand to Tillie. She took it.

"So no Lost and Found anymore?" he asked her.

"You heard, huh?"

"Well, I noticed you're missing your most prized appendage," Jake said.

"Yeah . . ." She felt like she couldn't even talk about it. "Things change, I guess. Hey, at least we're not mad at each other anymore."

"Yeah." He waved at her mom and her mom waved enthusiastically back.

"Sorry to disappoint your mom," he said to Tillie with a big smirk, "but I'm still not your boyfriend, so don't get any ideas."

Tillie smiled, and they took a few steps toward the car. "Well, what my mom says usually goes, so . . . sorry. You'll just have to accept our love."

"Poor Tom Wilson, then," Jake said, chuckling.

"What?!" Tillie stopped walking immediately.

"Oh, come on, you know Tom Wilson is in love with you, right?"

"Shut. Up."

"I'm serious!"

"You're so wrong. Tom Wilson is in love with Lauren Canopy. They write each other love notes!"

"What? Are you kidding me? They're best friends! They probably, like, took baths together as kids. Tillie, seriously? Those love notes he always asks you to look for? The notes you found so easily? They were for *you*! Lauren Canopy helps him write them! He hoped you would read them! Like any normal person would! Oh my God, I can't believe you didn't know this. And here I thought you were an *observer*." Jake cracked up, mouth wide in his typical guffaw, which Tillie hadn't seen in far too long.

"Shut up. Shut up, shut up, shut up." Tillie felt her face blush scarlet. "I have a limp!"

"Oh, I didn't realize that also meant you weren't a girl."

Tillie punched his arm. "Stop. I'm leaving."

As she climbed into the car, she heard Jake yell, "Have a lovely day, Mrs. Green!"

"Is everything okay?" her mom asked.

"Yeah," Tillie answered, turning to her. "Thanks, Mom."

Her mom's chin quivered. She put her hand to Tillie's cheek. "You got it, sweetheart," she said, tucking a strand of Tillie's hair behind her ear and out of her eyes.

"He's a nice boy," her mom said as she drove away.

"Yeah, Mom, I know," she said. "But we're just friends, okay?" Tillie smiled. "We're friends."

22

Found

SUNDAY CAME, AND SOMETHING HAD BEEN lifted. Maybe she was imagining it, but she could swear her foot hurt less when she put her weight on it as she stepped out of bed.

Tillie cracked open her window. It was almost May, and the air smelled fresh. Tillie's fingers itched to capture Sunday's morning light, which streamed through the branches of the trees with a melancholy beauty.

Tillie thought of her cameras, and closed her eyes, away from the window's sunbeams. Her poor cameras. They were so beautiful, and now they were trash.

Her bedroom door was open a crack and Tillie sensed someone there.

"Yeah?" she said.

Her dad knocked a little on the door even as he opened it and said, "Morning. Sorry to bother you."

"It's okay," she said, turning from the window to her dad. "I'm literally doing nothing."

He held something in his hand.

"It's been an . . . an odd month, huh?" he said.

"Yeah. I guess it has," she admitted.

Outside, the birds' chirping shifted from solos to chorus.

"Your teacher from the other day? Who called?" her dad said in his mumbling, awkward way.

"Yeah, Dad?"

"She's the one, huh?" he asked. "Miss M . . . something?"

He wasn't looking directly at Tillie as he spoke, but he looked toward her, toward the bed.

Tillie nodded.

"She described the photograph. The one for the art show?" He paused. "Is this it?" He pulled out the picture. Her dad, seemingly alone with his lunch. Tillie, reflected behind him. "I found it in the . . . in all the pictures that you took."

Tillie stared at it in his big hand. It was stacked on top of a couple of others. The glossy papers shook slightly in his grip.

"Yeah, that's it," she said. "It's really not very good, actually."

"Oh?" he said. He looked at it, squinting a little, as if trying to see it from her eyes. "I think it's good. I really think you should let her put your work in. Don't hide them from everyone, like Vivian Maier or something," he said, in what sounded like an attempt to be funny. He paused like he was waiting for her to respond, but she didn't, and then he went on. "She said that you turn in a lot of pictures of me. Those pictures of me that I found? Is that what they were for?" he asked.

"Partly," Tillie whispered. Her voice came out like she hadn't spoken in days—foggy and slow.

He paused and nodded. "Is the art show at school? Or . . ."

"Yeah."

"Oh, okay," he said. "Well, mind if I say something?"

"Yeah, sure," Tillie answered with apprehension.

"I really like the photo you took of me for the art show . . ."

"Yeah?" Tillie said. She felt a "but" coming.

"But do you think Ms. Martinez might still let you do the show if you chose another one?"

Tillie felt herself sink into the bed. She leaned back

against the wall. Maybe her dad wanted her to show her pictures, but not one from her "stalker" phase.

Her dad came farther into the room, standing right in front of her bed. "I'm sorry, but I took this from your room the other day. With the others. Maybe she'd let you use it instead," her dad said. "I really love it." He turned the photo toward her, and Tillie's own face stared back. It was the self-portrait she had taken the day Ms. Martinez drove her to the doctor's. Her mom had gotten it developed for her at Walmart a month or so ago, but Tillie had been so distracted by Jake's dad that she hadn't really taken it in.

In the image, Tillie stood in front of her closet's mirror with a camera at her chest, her face peering into its own reflection, questioning. The camera's strap slid slightly off one shoulder. Her foot stuck out to the side. Her stance, as always, fell lopsided. Her whole self, top to bottom, was visible. She still didn't know what story the picture told.

"Of all your photos, I think I like it the best," he said. "It's perfect."

Her dad said this like it was nothing.

"Dad," Tillie said, and she could not explain why she said this in this moment, "I broke my cameras."

Her dad's forehead crinkled, like a ratty old piece of balled-up paper. He glanced behind himself, past Tillie, through the walls toward where her mom was getting ready for the day, and then all around himself, like he was searching for the voice that might have said those words.

He started to speak, stopped, started again, stopped again, and then said, *"What?"*

Tillie shrugged.

"Well, wha—" he said. "Wait, you broke it?"

"Them. I broke *them*. Plural," she said. "The one grandpa gave me, too," she added.

Tillie's dad's face fell. Shocked, she saw that her dad appeared much more pained than he ever had standing at the kitchen window, watching the birds. He looked more upset than in any fight with her mom. He closed his eyes, and to Tillie his face didn't seem so unknowable anymore, but simply sad, and she really didn't think she could take it any longer, all that sadness, so she just spit out what she had realized when she was with Jake the other day. This thought that had bubbled up within her, in the midst of everyone being so mad at her.

"I'm not mad at you, Dad. Okay?" she said, looking right into his shut eyes, right into his fallen face. "I forgive you."

His eyes opened. The photos visibly shook in his hand.

"I just . . ." Tillie tried to continue. "So. I thought you should know."

Her dad looked down at his feet and said, with care, as if feeling things out, "Til, listen. I know I shouldn't have reacted by yelling about your pictures. I know. So, thanks for . . . I . . . What'd we say when you were a little kid? I 'accept your apology,' okay? I mean it. And I shouldn't have yelled."

His eyes darted downward, escaping her. He put a hand on his forehead.

"No, Dad. No, just . . . Look at me for a second, okay?" she said. Tillie felt her hair falling into her eyes. She pushed it away, placing it behind both shoulders. She looked straight at the man before her. She was seated on the bed as he stood, reminding her of how he used to stand, a bit apart, as her mom pushed her around in the wheelchair. "Look at me, Dad."

Her dad looked down, up, side to side, until he finally managed to point his head toward hers. He didn't look directly at her, but it was good enough. He stared at her forehead, maybe her cheeks, or her mouth, as that mouth spoke words she should have said long ago, if only she'd known they were the right ones.

"Dad," she continued slowly, feeling out the word as if she'd never really said it before. *"I forgive you."* She moved herself toward the edge of the bed and stood up next to him, facing him.

Tillie's dad surprised her by laughing abruptly. A short, high-pitched laugh.

"What's going on, Til?" he said.

Tillie fought the urge to pretend this wasn't happening, like Jake pretended things didn't happen. She couldn't do that. She didn't let her gaze go. Her gaze, unobstructed by the glass of a lens, frightened her, but it was still her most trusted skill and her best bet.

"I forgive you for the accident," she said. "Okay? I'm not mad. And I'm okay, Dad. I'm really okay. And," she took a breath, and repeated, *"I forgive you."* She exhaled. "I always have."

Tillie's leg started to hurt. She hadn't stretched yet, and she found herself leaning against the bed as she spoke to him.

She bit her lip.

Her dad stood there, his hands still at his sides. Silent.

"Ya know," she said offhandedly, like how Jake did when he was trying to lighten the mood, "everybody makes mistakes." She softened her voice completely.

"Right, Dad?" Tillie ventured, moving her head forward with a tilt, a little more toward him.

He remained quiet, staring down.

If she waited long enough, maybe he'd say something.

But he didn't.

Tillie's dad pressed his lips together tightly, as if maybe he was mad. Then he looked up at the ceiling, like someone does in a prayer, though she'd never seen her dad pray before. He rubbed his forehead and ran a hand through his hair.

Finally, with no words, he looked into her eyes.

"Thanks."

He let out a breath, as if he'd been holding it for four years, and his eyes smiled.

"And now I have to sit back on the bed," Tillie said. "I should stretch."

In a flash, her dad took her elbow like her mom used to when Tillie was recovering from the accident, and he helped her sit down. She needed absolutely zero help, but she let him do it. They both sat on her bed and leaned against the wall together, legs out.

Down the hall, in the kitchen, they heard her mom.

"Pancakes," Tillie said, right as her dad said it, too.

Tillie thought she heard him sniffle. But maybe it was nothing.

Tillie's dad pulled her close.

Slowly, carefully, Tillie laid her head on her dad's shoulder. Through his shoulder and the crease of his neck she could hear his heart beating. She felt his muscles stiffen, and then relax.

"Tillie," her dad said. She could hear the vibrations of her name through his skin.

"Yeah?" she said. She could hardly breathe. She felt the muscles in her palm start to twitch, and she hoped he didn't feel it, because then maybe he'd think she was uncomfortable, but really she felt like she was taking a warm shower after a chilly winter day.

"How about we go to the store?"

"Um," Tillie said, a question in her voice. "Okay . . ."

"To pick you up a new camera."

Tillie lifted her hand from his knee and put it to her chest.

"What?" she said, her head perking up and turning to him.

"How about we get you a new camera? Pick one out?"

It was like he had spoken gibberish.

"I don't know anything about this stuff," he said, his head bobbing slightly. "Is it not called a 'store' where you buy cameras? Is it a special kind of name? Like a 'camera shop'? Is there some lingo?" He was almost babbling now. "Anyway, I don't know what's good, so I can't really say, but I'm sure you know, right? You know all the good cameras." He rubbed his hair, shaking it so that it looked even messier. Tillie thought of Jake with his dandruff. "And let's not skimp on this." He seemed to be talking to himself. "I think we need one that makes up for all two or three—or whatever it was—of the broken cameras. So you can take pictures that are, you know, as good as possible. As good as you are."

Tillie stared at him.

"I mean, your photos are simply amazing, Tillie." He took a breath. His voice slowed down. "I've noticed." He breathed out, and she felt the heat of his breath on her shoulder. "I've *always* noticed," he added with de-liberation, articulating every syllable as he made an-other commendable attempt at prolonged eye contact. "I just . . ." And whatever else he had to say to her was still too hard. He exhaled. He lifted his hands and dropped them against his knees, as if giving up.

At her speechlessness, his forehead creased like he was

a kid who was worried people didn't like him, and he added, "We don't need to get one right away or anything."

Tillie's cheeks bumped up against the bottom rims of her glasses because she was smiling so widely.

"No, yes, now!" she said. "Let's go get Mom to take us! Now!" Tillie started to push herself up from his shoulders, and he stood to help her.

"Oh, no, no, it's okay," her dad said. "I'll drive you."

Tillie pretended she hardly heard this. But, for a second, she swore she could tap-dance all the way to New York City if she wanted to.

"Oh, okay," was what she said aloud, as casually as possible.

"I'll tell your mom."

Her dad went down the hall to the kitchen and adult voices spoke.

Alone, Tillie picked up her phone. Her mom had never taken it back from her, though Tillie knew it wasn't because she had forgotten. Her mom had forgiven her, too.

She texted Jake.

Dad's taking me to get a new camera . . . !!!

A few seconds later, as she tied her shoelaces, her screen read:

good morning to you too . . . u r the best lost and found ever. glad to have you back

Tillie smiled and tucked her phone in her pocket, on vibrate, in case Jake or Abby texted her to meet up later. She couldn't imagine she was still grounded.

When she got to the front door, the car keys were in her dad's hand. He had thrown on a light jacket.

Her mom stood leaning in the doorway in her robe. "You're missing out on pancakes."

"Sorry, Mom."

"Bye, you two. Have fun!" her mom said, way too cheerily.

Tillie and her dad stood at the door for a moment before her dad turned the doorknob, and they left.

As they walked toward the car, Tillie didn't know exactly what she'd found, but she knew she'd found something. And with that wonderfully vague certainty, feeling the sweet, warming air graze across her face through the open car window, her dad putting in the key and turning on the radio, Tillie said goodbye to her old eyes. She let them close. She knew that this search was over, that when she opened her eyes again she would have a brand-new lens with which to see the world. With her eyes closed, Tillie thought of all she'd already found, and all that was left to find.

"You ready?" her dad said.

"Absolutely," Tillie replied, her eyes opening to see him smile at her.

And he put the car in drive.

Acknowledgments

Thank you to the team at Roaring Brook Press for the incredible support. Thank you to my gifted editor, Connie Hsu, for sharing your brilliance with me, to Noa Wheeler for your sensitive insights, to Megan Abbate for those great pep talks, and to Kylie Byrd and Jennifer Sale for your impeccable attention to detail.

Thank you to my extraordinary agent, Melissa Edwards, for fighting so hard for this book. You are a gem.

Thank you to Boyoun Kim for gracing the cover with such lovely art, and to Christina Dacanay for designing a beautiful book.

Thank you to Sara Polsky for helping me dive deeper into Tillie's world.

Eternal thanks to Pamela Laskin for guiding me through the early stages of the manuscript.

Thank you to Jenna Werner, Nick Shoda, Rachel Mylan, Gabriel Frye-Behar, Arin Sang-urai, and Kelly Granito for your time and expertise.

Thank you to the only real mermaid I've ever met, Tillie Spencer, for sparking this story in my imagination.

Thank you to Lexi Lessaris for all the precious writing hours, and for the gift of your warmth.

Endless gratitude to my high school creative writing teacher, Community High School's Tracy Anderson. You helped me discover my love of writing and consistently demonstrated a belief in the importance of each student's voice, including mine. You are everything a teacher should be.

Thank you to Jacob M. Appel, who convinced me to pursue writing and showed me that living a writer's life is worth it. Your talent and perseverance inspire me.

To my big, beautiful family, near and far, whose love grounds me.

Thank you to Lizzie and Robert Gottlieb for all the advice.

Thank you to my late grandma, Alice Brady, who taught me how to tell a good story.

Thank you to my dad, Ernest P. Young, for the countless hours you've spent poring over this and every other manuscript.

Thank you to my mom, M. Brady Mikusko, for supporting me wholeheartedly in any career path I wanted, from early dreams of becoming a botanist/orca specialist/actress to this realized one of writing books, embodying the philosophy of raising a child to follow her heart.

Thank you to my other mom and dad, Margery and David Ross, for the constant encouragement. You are the fan club every person needs!

Thank you to my nephews, Oliver Young and Jacob Young, for allowing me to pick your brains endlessly about what it is to be twelve years old in the world today. You guys are the future we need.

Thank you to my niece, Claudia Maschio, whose exuberance nourishes me.

Thank you to my darling Simone. You are joy.

And, of course, thank you to Jonathan Ross, my love. Let's never stop swapping drafts and ideas and jokes. Especially the jokes.